BLOOD IN THE VALLEY

HARRY STARKE THE EARLY YEARS

HARRY STARKE GENESIS
BOOK 9

BLAIR HOWARD

Print ISBN: 979-8-9908529-8-3
Printed Cleveland, TN, USA

For Jo
As Always

PROLOGUE

It was a little after nine on the evening of October 15, 2006. It was also the 150th anniversary celebration of the "prestigious" Volunteer Valley Country Club, and I use the word prestigious with a certain amount of... cynicism. Exclusive? Yes. Snobby? Certainly. The members were, for the most part, also members of Chattanooga's and Hamilton County's elite, of which I'm also counted a member, and of the old Chattanooga Country Club where I'm much more comfortable.

So why was I there? I was there because I'm a member and because it's where the action was, and I don't mean the golf. I mean, it's where the movers and shakers go about their business, their plotting, and their drinking. I was, after all, a police officer, a detective sergeant attached to the Homicide Division of the Chattanooga PD, though I must admit I was a wealthy cop, old money too, which is why I was accepted there, though looked down upon by some because of my chosen profession. And it didn't hurt that my father, August, was, back then, a multi-millionaire; today, the old sweat is a billionaire, thanks to a very successful class action lawsuit. Yes, he's a lawyer.

And so, with a glass of expensive scotch in hand, I watched Elizabeth Rawlings from my spot at the bar, studying how Chattanooga's elite moved around her like schools of expensive fish. The flickering light of the crystal chandeliers caught in her silver hair, still regal and fit as the proverbial fiddle at seventy-four, as she clutched a leather portfolio–the one containing the plans that would reshape Chattanooga's North Shore and, though I didn't know it yet, expose generations of buried secrets.

The Masons, though, kept to their corner table, watching, talking softly among themselves. Old man Thomas's weathered face was a mask of indifference. Only his white-knuckled grip on his glass of bourbon betrayed any latent hostility.

"She's going to announce it tonight," Kate murmured, appearing at my elbow. "The development project everyone's been whispering about."

Kate Gazzara, also a detective sergeant, was my partner at work and in life. She looked stunning in a black, sleeveless, ankle-length sheath and black four-inch heels, her blonde hair curled down around her shoulders framing her beautiful face. I, of course, being the gentleman that I was, murmured, "Geez, Kate, is it just me, or did it suddenly get a lot hotter in here?"

"That, Sergeant, is a lop-sided compliment if ever I heard one," she replied. "I take it you approve."

"Oh yeah," I said. "I so approve, and…" It was at that moment I caught old man Mason's eye, but he quickly looked away. I nodded in his direction and whispered, "Look at Mason. Who kicked his dog? I wonder. He looks like he's at a funeral, not an anniversary party. What would you like to drink?"

"I think…" She paused and smiled at me. "…Champagne?"

I smiled, nodded, and turned to the bartender and said, "A bottle of Dom Perignon 2002, please."

The bartender, deadpan, turned, bent down and grabbed a bottle from a shelf I couldn't see, popped the cork, poured some into a glass, looked at me and said, "For the lady, I presume, sir?"

I nodded, and he set the glass down in front of Kate and the bottle on the bar where he could maintain control of it.

I smiled at him, tilted my head a little and said, "Thank you, Marvin. Add twenty percent to the tab for yourself." And there it was at last, just the hint of a smile as he nodded and turned away. *No thank you.* I thought. *Oh well, look where we are.*

The club president rose and made a somewhat lengthy introduction which drew polite applause, and Elizabeth Rawlings stood, inclined her head to acknowledge it, and then, glass in hand, moved to the lectern with unhurried steps, the portfolio held close beneath her arm. The emeralds at her throat—a Rawlings heirloom that had survived the Great Depression when so many other fortunes hadn't—flashed as she walked.

She cleared her throat, took a drink from the glass, looked around at the gathered dignitaries, and blinked several times. "For one hundred and fifty years," she began, her voice strong without even a hint of a quaver despite her age, "this club has witnessed the growth of our city. Tonight, we stand at another crossroads." She opened the portfolio and looked down at it. "The North Shore project will—"

She faltered. Took a small step back. The crystal glass slipped from her fingers. She clutched the lectern with her free hand. Her face turned ashen. I leaped to my feet, moving before she began to fall, but Kate reached her first.

The emeralds clicked against one another as Elizabeth convulsed. Her portfolio slipped from her fingers, papers scattered, floating across the polished boards. I helped Kate lower her gently to the floor and, as I cradled her head, I caught a whiff of bitter almonds.

"Call an ambulance!" Kate shouted, checking her vitals. I looked at her and shook my head. I was very familiar with cyanide poisoning, and I knew she'd be dead within minutes.

The crowd surged forward, smartphones appearing like fireflies. I waved them back. James Rawlings III pushed through, dropped to one knee beside his grandmother, and took her hand in both of his. Thomas Mason remained seated, a slight smile on his lips, but only for a second, and then his expression turned sour, as if he, too, had caught the scent of bitter almonds.

Elizabeth clutched my sleeve and whispered, "Ask about the fire of '47." They were her last words.

Her right hand relaxed. Her fingers opened, releasing a crumpled photograph. I grabbed it and tucked it away in my jacket pocket before anyone noticed, my instincts telling me it was important.

I stood up and shouted for everyone to go back to their seats, that the ballroom was now a crime scene. The paramedics arrived ten minutes later and confirmed what I already knew; Elizabeth Rawlings was dead, and I, being the first and most senior officer on the scene, had caught the case.

After ensuring everyone was settled, I went to a quiet corner, took the photo from my pocket, and studied it. It was an image of two families posed proudly together before a Victorian mansion on Cameron Hill. The Rawlings and the Masons stood together, their wealth and power clear in every starched collar and black silk dress. I turned it over. The date on the back read "September 14, 1947."

Kate joined me a moment later. "I bagged and tagged the water glass," she said. "I put it in the car. It smells of cyanide. But here's the thing; it was her glass. She brought it with her. Her chauffer says she went nowhere without it. He said she called it her lucky glass."

I glanced at the photograph again. I knew a little of the families' history. I knew that just one day after this picture was taken, something had shattered the bond between these two families. The next week, the Mason textile mill burned to the ground. Now, three generations later, I had no doubt that Elizabeth Rawlings had been murdered, and that she'd died with a secret on her lips and evidence in her hands.

"What's that?" Kate asked, nodding at the photograph.

"History," I replied. "History coming back to haunt us. Look at him," I said, as I watched Thomas Mason being interviewed by uniformed officers, his composure finally cracking. "There's a lot of history and a lot of bad blood between those two families. And I've got a feeling we're about to learn just how deep it goes."

At the far side of the ballroom, I could see James Rawlings III was also watching Mason, his eyes narrowed to mere slits. His hatred plain for all to see, and no wonder. Doc Sheddon had spent less than five minutes examining the body before ordering it removed to his little house of horror.

The scattered papers, the development plans—I already knew —confirmed the massive changes coming to the North Shore. But now, upon Elizabeth's death, I suspected the real changes would come from whatever it was she'd discovered about that long-ago fire. I suspected it was a secret worth killing to protect.

And I had one of those inexplicable feelings deep in my gut that was telling me. In her last moments, Elizabeth Rawlings had handed me the evidence that would launch a probe that would expose... What? Well, of course, I didn't know then, but I soon would.

.

1

IT WAS LATE when I arrived home that night. I have a condo on Lakeshore Lane overlooking the river. Kate had elected to go home to her apartment in East Brainerd, so I spent a few moments in my living room watching the lights of the Thrasher Bridge reflecting off the quiet waters of the Tennessee. It was something I often did when I needed to unwind. And unwind I did, but I still woke early the following morning feeling as if I'd been put through a woodchipper.

It was still dark outside when I slipped out of bed and went downstairs to make coffee, then back up again and took a quick shower. Suitably refreshed, I dressed in jeans and a white golf shirt, then I went downstairs again, made two slices of sourdough toast, poured myself a cup of coffee, turned on the TV in the kitchen and then sat down at the table to eat.

The local news channels were all carrying the story of Elizabeth Rawlings' apparent murder; none of them had it right. I flipped through the channels one after another, shaking my head at the speculative theories proffered by the morning anchors. I finally settled on Channel 7 and Amanda Cole. There was something about that woman that fascinated me, but that was before she did the hatchet job on me.

I hadn't been seated more than a few minutes, and was less than halfway into my coffee, when my phone buzzed. I didn't have to look at it to know who it was.

"Good morning, Chief," I said with a brightness I didn't feel.

"My office, Sergeant," the gravelly voice said. "Thirty minutes. Don't be late."

"As if—" I began, but he'd already hung up.

Ten minutes later, I rose from the table, washed my cup and plate and set them to drain, clipped my badge and department issue Glock 22 to my belt and slipped into a dark blue suit jacket. A quick glance in the hall mirror and I managed to persuade myself I was ready for the day. I nodded, checked my watch—it was just after eight—and walked out into the garage.

I opened the garage door to what was going to be a bright, sunshiny day. Sunshine or not, it was still a cold forty-five degrees outside.

I drove my unmarked Crown Victoria out onto the street, watching the garage door close behind me, then circled up onto Dupont Parkway and from there to the PD on Amnicola Highway, a drive of about ten minutes depending on the traffic, of course.

I arrived in Chief Wesley Johnston's outer office at twenty-seven minutes after eight, grinning to myself to find Kate already there.

"You, too?" I said.

She nodded, but didn't reply.

"Morning, Cindy," I said to his secretary. "Is the mighty one ready for us?"

Chapter 1

She smiled up at me, picked up the desk phone, tapped a button, and said, "Sergeants Starke and Gazzara are here."

She listened for a moment, then hung up and said, "You can go in. Be careful. He's not in the best of moods."

"When is he ever?" I asked.

I knocked once, opened the door, and stood aside for Kate to enter, then I followed her in and closed the door.

"Sit down, both of you," Johnston said without looking up from the report he was reading.

I looked at Kate and grinned as we sat side by side in the two wingback chairs in front of his desk.

Chief Wesley Johnston was, and still is, someone you don't mess with. Not over tall—five-tenish—hefty, but not fat, always impeccably dressed, his uniform pressed, his head shaved, he was an imposing figure. But it was his unusual mustache that really set him apart: think Hulk Hogan, and just as white. He was self-assured, not arrogant, but he did expect obedience from his officers and staff, to which I can personally attest. And, as far as I knew, he totally lacked a sense of humor. To this day, I don't think I've ever seen him even smile.

Cindy was right. He wasn't in a good mood but, fortunately, his right-hand man, an idiot by the name of Lieutenant Jack "Bull" Marshall, was absent.

After a long, silent moment, he set the report aside, locked his hands together in front of him on the desk, looked up, gave Kate a cursory glance, then looked at his watch and then glared at me and said, "By the skin of your teeth, Starke."

I smiled at him, giving him a good look at my teeth—teeth that had cost my mother an arm and a leg, bless her, but I didn't reply.

He stared at me thoughtfully for a moment, then said, "Elizabeth Rawlings?" It was a statement as much as it was a question.

I nodded, "We're waiting for the autopsy report, but I'm pretty sure she was poisoned, cyanide."

"Suspects?" he asked.

I shook my head and said, "As of now, none, but we'll get there."

He nodded and seemed to lighten up a little. "I'm sure you will, Harry, but time is not of the essence. I've already had the mayor on the phone this morning and the press is all over it. What's your plan?"

"My plan, Chief, is to conduct the investigation as I would any other investigation, methodically and diligently. Just because the victim is a local dignitary, it doesn't mean we have to go after it half-assed."

His expression hardened, then relaxed. It obviously wasn't what he wanted to hear, but he knew I'd get the job done.

He stared at me for a moment, then nodded and said, "As I would expect, Harry. What d'you need from me?"

I looked at Kate. She inclined her head slightly, but said nothing.

"Support and backup when we need it and..." I locked eyes with him, "keep Bull off my back. He's more hinderance than help."

Is that the hint of a smile? I wondered as I watched his eyes narrow ever so slightly. *Nah!*

"Lieutenant Marshall speaks for me," he said. "You'll report to me daily, by phone or in person, before five-thirty. Keep your nose clean, Harry." He looked at Kate and said, "Keep him in line, Sergeant."

At that, Kate smiled. "I'll do my best, Chief."

He nodded, then said, "That is all." And the interview was over.

"I'm starving," I said as I closed the outer office door behind us. "Let's go get something to eat."

Chapter 1

"So, where do we start?" Kate asked between mouthfuls of sausage and egg biscuit.

"At the beginning," I replied. "At the crime scene. It's properly secured, right?"

She nodded, swallowed, and said, "Yep, ten uniforms and two K-9s." She looked at her watch. "Shift changed an hour ago. Mike Willis and his team were there all night. They left at eight. Oh, and Doc called. He's doing the post this afternoon. He wanted to know who's going to attend."

I grinned at her over my coffee.

"Yeah. That's what I thought," she said, dryly.

"My place after?" I asked.

She nodded. "You cooking?"

I shook my head. "Nah! I'll pick something up. Chinese sound okay?"

She pulled a face, then shrugged, "Yeah, I suppose." She looked again at her watch and said, "Time to go, Harry."

We arrived at the crime scene at a little after nine-forty-five to find the parking lot taped off and empty but for a half-dozen blue and white cruisers, a crime scene truck, and two black SUVs I didn't recognize.

A uniformed officer guarding the tape held up his hand, peered in at me, grinned and said, "You're good, Sarge."

I nodded to the SUVs. "Who do they belong to?"

"Victim's family," he replied as he stepped back and held up the tape for me to drive through.

I parked close to the entrance and Kate and I stepped out into the watery sunshine.

I looked around, then headed up the steps, through the double doors and into the foyer where we were met by a uniformed sergeant, Henry Pierce.

"Harry," he said, offering me his hand. "I heard you'd caught this one; you and Kate, that is."

"Hello, Henry," I said, taking his hand, briefly. "Anything to report?"

"Rawlings Junior's in the ballroom. Couldn't keep him out without restraining him. Thought it better not to do that, so I assigned an officer to keep an eye on him with strict instructions to keep him away from the crime scene."

"You should have restrained him," I said, "but I get it. You probably did the right thing. We'll talk later, okay?"

He nodded, and we made our way along the hallway and into the Volunteer Valley Country Club Grand Ballroom, though in daylight it didn't seem quite so grand as it had the previous evening.

The cold winter sunshine streamed in through the tall windows, casting long shadows across the crime scene. The great room felt hollow now, its elegance diminished by the lack of people and death's recent visit.

James Rawlings III, with Officer Mike Taplow standing nearby with his back to the wall, was pacing slowly back and forth, his Italian loafers clicking against the hardwood. At thirty-four, he had the polished look of old money, but it was obvious to both of us that grief had cracked his carefully crafted veneer.

Every few steps, he'd glance at the spot where his grandmother had collapsed, then resume his restless pacing, head down, hands in his pants pockets.

"Go check the security footage," I said to Kate. "I'll join you in a minute, after I've had a word with young Rawlings."

She nodded and headed back down the hall.

"Oh, there you are," Rawlings said as he looked up and stopped pacing. "About damn time. It was the Masons," he ran his perfectly manicured fingers through his carefully styled hair. "Has to be," he continued. "Three generations of sabotage, hostile takeovers, social backstabbing... and now this." His voice cracked slightly on the last word.

He was, I knew, thirty-four. Tall, athletic, narrow face, clean-shaven, with dark brown hair and piercing hazel eyes. He was wearing maroon colored golf pants and a white polo shirt under a monogrammed golf jacket.

"Walk me through last night," I said, without pre-amble, watching his reflection in the wall of windows overlooking the golf course. "Who had access to her water glass?"

"Everyone," he replied. "She brought it from home. She always used it at events like this. Called it her lucky glass." He laughed bitterly. "Some luck." He turned to face me. "But Thomas Mason was lurking around all evening. Ask my security people. He was everywhere she was, watching her."

"And you?" I asked.

"I was here, too, of course, all evening until..." he trailed off, staring out the window.

All of this I already knew, of course, having been seated at the bar watching the proceedings.

"Who refilled her glass?" I asked.

He shrugged. "How the hell should I know? I don't keep tabs on what the help is doing."

There were a great many more questions I could have asked him, but I already knew most of the answers, so I nodded and said, "Don't go anywhere, Mr. Rawlings. I may want to talk with you again." And, without waiting for an answer, I turned away and went to find Kate.

I found her in the security office surrounded by monitors, scanning the previous night's feeds. On the main screen, Thomas Mason, moving with surprising agility for his age, entered the wine cellar at seven-twenty-six and came out again nine minutes later, ninety minutes before Elizabeth's collapse.

"Other than this, there's nothing suspicious," Kate murmured, making notes. "There are no cameras down there, but the cellar also has access to the kitchen storage areas. Watch this." She reversed the footage. "He knew exactly where the cameras were. Never shows his face directly. Why was he down there?"

"We need to ask him," I said. "Let's go talk to the staff."

The staff interviews filled the next two hours with service industry gossip and carefully worded non-answers. The wait staff had seen nothing unusual. The bartenders remembered everyone's drinks, but nothing suspicious. The kitchen staff had been too busy to notice anything beyond their immediate tasks.

But something caught my eye in the main hallway. Someone had recently rearranged the historical photographs—the club's pride and joy. Gaps where frames had been moved showed dark patterns, and one spot, labeled 1947, was conspicuously empty.

"Harry, I need you in here," Kate called from the admin office.

"I found something interesting in Elizabeth's recent appointments. Three meetings in the past month with a Dr. Marcus Walker. He's a history professor at UTC. He specializes in Southern industrial families."

I frowned. "What the hell kind of history is that?"

"Industrial development, family dynasties, economic power structures prior to and during World War II." Kate replied as she pulled up his university profile. "He's published several books about Southern industry's role in the war effort."

I nodded. "I need out of here," I said. "Let's pay him a visit. Lunch first, though."

2

NEW BLOOD

Afternoon, October 16

IT WAS a little after two when we arrived at UTC where we found Dr. Walker in his office, surrounded by archives of Chattanooga's industrial past. He was sixtyish, with wire-rimmed glasses and an air of distracted intensity. His daughter Sarah was helping him sort through some old photographs when we arrived.

"Dr. Walker," I said, smiling and offering him my hand, "I'm Sergeant Starke, Chattanooga PD, and this is my partner, Sergeant Gazzara. D'you have a few minutes? We'd like to talk to you about Elizabeth Rawlings."

He glanced at his daughter, then back at me. "Of course. This is my daughter, Sarah. She's the university archivist, a somewhat dusty, if not interesting job, don't you think? Well… you wouldn't know about that, would you? Silly question. Please forgive me and… well, sit down."

We sat down at the over-large table opposite him.

"Now," he said, beaming. "I heard what happened to her. So

sad. Brilliant woman. A great friend of mine. She'll be sorely missed. What would you like to know?"

"You met with her five times during the past few weeks," I said. "What was that about?"

"Research," he said, and looked away.

I frowned. "What kind of research?"

"Elizabeth was researching something specific," Walker said, carefully choosing his words. He gestured for Sarah to leave, which she did reluctantly. "The connection between... certain families," he continued, "and... events during the war years. World War II, that is..." Again, he trailed off and looked away.

"The war years?" Kate asked.

"Yes," he replied. "Though she was particularly interested in the mill fire of 1947... Give me a moment." He stood, went to a file cabinet, and took out a file. He returned to the table, sat down, opened it and took out a photograph—taken the same year as the one missing from the country club's wall—and handed it to me. It showed both families together, posed in front of their Cameron Hill mansions.

"She was also researching the two families' financial activities just before America entered the war."

I studied the photograph. The Rawlings and Masons stood together, seemingly friendly. "When was this taken?"

"One day before everything changed, apparently," Walker said quietly. "One day before a seemingly profitable partnership turned into a feud. Or at least, appeared to turn into one."

"What do you mean, appeared?" Kate asked.

Walker glanced at the door through which his daughter had left. He was obviously uncomfortable. "Perhaps we should continue this discussion tomorrow. I need to... organize my research first. There are some things I need to verify before I make any statements."

I pursed my lips and stared at him.

He raised his chin in defiance.

I held his gaze for a moment, then capitulated. "Very well, Doctor. Tomorrow. Shall we say nine o'clock?"

"That would be fine," He replied. "Now, if you'll excuse me, I have a lot to do."

"WHAT NOW?" Kate asked, as she strapped herself in.

"Back to the club, I guess," I replied as I started the engine.

Back at the club, James Rawlings was still pacing.

"Where the hell have you been?" He snapped as we approached. "You told me not to leave, then you go off on some wild expedition. D'you think I have all day? I don't."

"I'm sorry," Kate said. "Something came up—"

"And who the hell are you?" he snapped.

"I'm Sergeant Kate Gazzara, Mr. Rawlings," she replied, "Sergeant Starke's partner. If you'll give us a few more minutes, we'll see if we can get you out of here. Now—"

"My grandmother was going to announce something big," he snapped, interrupting her. "The development project, yes, that, but something else, too. Something about our families' history."

"Did she tell you what it was?" I asked, frowning. His statement played into what we'd learned from Dr. Walker.

"No." He turned and stared out the window. "But the night before, I heard her talking to someone on the phone. She said, 'The feud was always a lie.' I don't know what she meant by that or who she was talking to."

The sun was setting when Kate and I finally left the club. We stopped at our usual coffee spot overlooking the river.

"The missing photograph," Kate said, reviewing her notes. "Walker's research. Elizabeth's meetings. It all points to something that happened in 1947."

"Yeah," I agreed, watching the lights come on along the riverfront. "And someone's willing to kill to keep that something buried. Her last words to me were, 'Ask about the fire of '47.' Walker mentioned that, too."

A text lit up my phone: *Country Club. Storage room B, basement level. Come alone.* It was from James Rawlings III.

I handed Kate my phone. She glanced at it and handed it back to me. "You going?" she asked.

"We are," I said as I stood.

"He said come alone," she said as she also stood.

"Yeah, well," I replied. "He doesn't make the rules. We do."

The country club's basement corridors were a maze of storage rooms and maintenance areas. The air smelled of old wood and expensive wine, with an undertone of something less pleasant. My flashlight beam caught gleaming bottles in the wine cellar where Thomas Mason had been caught by the security cameras.

"James?" I called out, keeping my back to the wall. No answer.

Storage room B was tucked away in a dark corner of the basement, its door slightly ajar. A sliver of light spilled out. I nodded to Kate, pulled the door open and stepped inside to find not James, but Margaret Mason, Thomas's granddaughter. She was standing by a filing cabinet, her black designer pant suit incongruous in the dusty room.

"Sergeant Starke," she said, her voice controlled but tense. "You brought a friend, I see."

"My partner, Sergeant Gazzara," I replied. "Where's James?"

"I borrowed his phone," she replied. "He doesn't know I'm here. We need to talk."

She was a small woman, not more than five seven in her three-inch heels, blonde with a heart-shaped face, heavily made up. The suit she was wearing probably cost more than a compact car.

"About Elizabeth?" I asked.

"About what she found." Margaret pulled a manila envelope from the cabinet. "And about why both our families are terrified she found it."

Before she could continue, footsteps echoed in the corridor. Margaret quickly shoved the envelope back into the cabinet. James Rawlings III appeared in the doorway, looking first surprised, then angry.

"What are you doing here?" he demanded, glaring at Margaret.

"Same as you," she replied. "Damage control."

The tension between them felt rehearsed, like actors performing familiar roles. Something about their hostility rang false.

"Your grandmother," she said to James, "was going to destroy everything. Both of our families."

"By announcing a development project?" I asked.

They exchanged a look that spoke volumes. "The project was just her cover," James said finally. "What she really found…" He stopped as his phone buzzed. The color drained from his face as he read the message.

"They found something at the construction site," he said to Margaret. Their feigned animosity vanished instantly, replaced by what appeared to be shared panic.

"We have to go," Margaret said, as she grabbed the manila file and hurried past me. James followed without another word, their sudden cooperation more telling than their sham rivalry.

Kate's phone rang. "Hello," she said. "He what…? When…? They want what…? D'you know who— I see… Just one or both? I —" She took the phone from her ear, looked at it and said, "Damn it. She hung up." She looked at me and continued, "That was Sarah Walker. She says her father's been receiving threats. Someone wants his research on the families."

"Both families?" I asked.

"The threats came from a single source that claims to represent both the Rawlings and Mason's interests."

The pieces were starting to form a pattern, but not the one anyone would have expected. The legendary feud between two of

Chattanooga's greatest families was beginning to look like an elaborate performance.

My phone buzzed, a text from Dr. Walker. He was asking to meet, and it was urgent.

Kate and I headed back up to ground level and then out into the parking lot. The evening air was heavy with approaching rain.

"You know what's strange?" Kate said, as we drove to the university. "Everyone keeps talking about this feud, but I've never seen two enemies work so hard to protect each other's secrets."

She was right. It was as if we were watching a carefully choreographed dance, and I figured Elizabeth Rawlings was about to stop the music, and she'd paid with her life.

The question was: how many more would die before the dance finally ended?

The drive to UTC took us past the North Shore development site about which Elizabeth Rawlings had planned to make her announcement. The construction equipment stood silent in the gathering dusk, yellow machines turned to gold by the setting sun, and I couldn't help but wonder if it was something about the site that had spooked both James and Margaret enough to make them drop their pretense of rivalry.

"Pull over," Kate blurted, "look." She pointed to a figure hurrying across the campus parking lot. It was Sarah Walker, carrying a heavy box of files.

We caught up with her at her father's office door. She looked distraught, her hands shaking slightly as she fumbled with the keys.

"Dad's not here," she said, glancing nervously over her shoulder. "He said he had to check something in the historical society archives. Something about the mill fire."

"The 1947 fire?" I asked.

She nodded, finally getting the door open. "He's been obsessed with it since Elizabeth first visited him. He said it's the key to everything; whatever that means." She set the box down on her father's cluttered desk. "There was something wrong with him this morning. He was different. Scared. He said if anything happened to him, I should give these to you."

She put a hand on the box and lifted the lid. It contained photographs, documents, a leather-bound journal and, on top, a newspaper clipping about the Mason mill fire, its headline yellowed with age.

"Dad said Elizabeth had found proof it wasn't an accident," Sarah continued. "He said both families worked together to set the fire, then blamed each other publicly. It was all theater."

"Theater?" Kate asked. "To what end?"

Before Sarah could answer, her phone chimed. The color drained from her face as she read the message.

"It's from the security company," she said. "There's been a break in at the historical society," she whispered. "Dad's not there. No one's there."

I nodded to Kate. She took out her phone to call it in while I picked up the journal and checked the most recent entries. Dr. Walker had documented and made notes of his meetings with Elizabeth Rawlings. The last entry was underlined twice: "The feud is fake." Everything we thought we knew about these two families is wrong."

"We need to find your father," I told Sarah. "Where else might he have gone?"

"The old newspaper archives at the university library, maybe? Or…" She stopped, realizing something. "The mill site. He said Elizabeth had found something in the original foundations. Something that survived the fire."

"Let's go," I snapped.

Thunder rumbled overhead as we rushed back to the car. The first heavy drops of rain hit the windshield as we pulled out of the parking lot. Behind us, the university's lights blurred in the gathering storm.

We were halfway there when Kate's scanner crackled to life. A security guard at the construction site had called in what he thought was suspicious activity near the old mill site, multiple figures.

"They must have followed him," Sarah said, her voice tight with fear. "They must have tracked him somehow."

The rain was falling in sheets now, turning Chattanooga's streets into gleaming rivers of light from the streetlamps. I drove on through the rain, certain that somewhere up ahead, Dr. Walker was about to discover why some questions were better left unasked.

The construction site loomed ahead; skeletal machinery silhouetted against the stormy sky. The gate hung open, lock and chain dangling. Deep tire tracks in the mud showed where multiple vehicles had recently entered.

"There," Kate said, pointing.

Off to the right, I could see flashlight beams dancing near the pit where the old mill foundations lay exposed.

I killed the lights and parked behind a stack of concrete pipes. Sarah opened the door and started to get out, but I stopped her. "Stay here. Call campus security, tell them where your father went, and ask them to check the newspaper archives. Kate, you call for backup."

The rain hammered down as Kate and I moved quickly toward the pit, weapons drawn. As we drew closer, we could hear voices, at least four people, and they were arguing.

"They have to be here somewhere," a male voice insisted. It sounded like James Rawlings III. "Walker said Elizabeth had found proof here, in the foundations."

"Spread out," a female voice ordered. *Margaret Mason?* I wondered. "Check every corner. We need those papers before—"

A sudden shout cut through the rain. Dr. Walker's voice, triumphant, cutting Rawlings off: "You're too late! I've already made copies. I photographed everything and sent it all to a secure location."

I heard the sound of running feet. A flashlight beam swung wildly, momentarily illuminating Walker's face as he emerged from behind a concrete pylon, clutching what looked like an old metal box to his chest.

Then everything happened at once.

Private security officers materialized from the shadows; some with Rawlings patches visible on their tactical gear, some with Mason. They appeared to be working together, just as Sarah Walker had said. Was the feud indeed theater?

"Dad!" Sarah's scream cut through the sound of the wind and rain. She'd left the car and was running toward her father.

Gunfire erupted, sharp cracks competing with the thunder. Walker was hit, and went down hard. The metal box flew through the air to land in the mud close to the edge of the pit.

"Call for an ambulance," I yelled at Kate.

Sarah reached her father first and together we dragged him behind a stack of rusting rebar.

The security team was gone as quickly as it had appeared, melting into the darkness. James Rawlings and Margaret Mason had also vanished, but I could hear their voices carrying back on the wind. "This is your damn family's fault!"

"No, it wasn't. It was yours!"

Walker was alive, but barely. Sarah cradled his head as we heard sirens approaching.

"The box," he gasped. "Don't let them…" He trailed off.

But the metal box was gone, either taken or fallen back into the pit now rapidly filling with rainwater. Whatever Elizabeth had found in the mill foundations would stay hidden a while longer. *I wonder what the hell he did with the photographs.*

Later, at the hospital, they were able to stabilize Walker, but he was unwilling to talk. Sarah shared one last thing as we left:

"Dad said Elizabeth found something else. Something bigger

than the mill fire. She hid the evidence somewhere in the development plans themselves."

I thanked her, and we left her standing there, miserable and wet.

The storm was passing as Kate and I headed back downtown.

"Two attempts to kill people who knew too much," Kate said. "First Elizabeth Rawlings, now Walker. What the hell is going on, Harry?"

"Two attempts," I said, "plus Walker's missing box and the missing photo at the country club. Someone's systematically erasing the evidence of… something."

"And the feud that's divided Chattanooga society for three generations…?" she trailed off.

"…is looking more like a cover story every minute," I finished for her. "I'm bushed," I said. "Let's go home. We can pick up something to eat along the way. Sound good?"

She nodded. "Not Chinese. I feel kind of queasy. Maybe a wrap from Lester's."

We spent the evening together on the couch in front of the floor-to-ceiling window, watching the river. The storm was over, but the Tennessee was moody that night, the water sometimes smooth, sometimes choppy. It matched my own mood. Kate was also uncharacteristically quiet. By ten-thirty, we were both nodding, so we called it a night and went to bed.

THE FIRE
Afternoon, Wednesday, October 17

KATE and I rose early the following day and after a four-mile run and a minimal breakfast of toast and jam, we spent the morning in the situation room at the PD, Kate doing background checks and me delving into the history of the two families. By noon, we'd both had enough and decided to go to lunch just down the road at the Boathouse.

And so it was that by two o'clock that afternoon we were sitting side-by-side in the university archives, staring at two microfiche readers. I was scrolling through sixty-year-old copies of the Chattanooga Times, searching for answers about the 1947 mill fire, while Kate was doing the same with the Chattanooga Free Press.

"Got it. Here," Kate said, pointing to the screen. MASON MILL DESTROYED IN MIDNIGHT BLAZE.

The article painted a brutal picture. Chattanooga's largest textile mill had been reduced to ashes. Three night watchmen had died in the fire. Thomas Mason Sr.'s empire had crumbled overnight. Within weeks, Rawlings Steel had swooped in, buying the land for pennies on the dollar.

Dr. Walker's words echoed in my mind as I studied the grainy photos: "The feud is fake. Everything we thought we knew about these families is wrong."

My phone buzzed. I looked at the screen. It was Sarah Walker calling from her father's hospital room. "Dad's awake," she said. "But there's something else. I found his research notes about the fire. Harry… the night watchmen that were killed, they weren't supposed to be there. Someone changed the schedule at the last minute."

Okay, I thought. *So what does that mean?*

But before I could respond, Kate found another article. Two days after the fire, both families had attended a charity gala together. The photos showed them smiling, cordial, only hours before the bitter feud supposedly began.

"Thanks for calling, Sarah. I'll get back to you soon." I disconnected the call then said to Kate, "I think it's time we talked to Thomas Mason and see what he remembers about his father's 'enemy.'"

THE MASON ESTATE was perched on Missionary Ridge like a fading crown, its limestone facade weathered by decades of watching over a city that had slowly slipped from its grasp. As you'd expect, the gardens were immaculate. After all, old money never lets appearances slip, even in decline.

"You go take a look around the outside while I go talk to the old man," I said.

She nodded and walked away to the south while I looked up at the façade and shook my head. My family was wealthy, but this pre-Civil War relic with its doric columns and balconies was, to me, more than a little over the top.

Before I reached the top step of a dozen, the door opened and I was met by the Mason's English butler, Reginald.

"Mr. Thomas is awaiting you in his study, Mr. Starke," he said, then turned away and said, "If you'll follow me, please."

Is he now? I thought. *I wonder how he knew I was coming.*

Thomas Mason was standing—perhaps I should say posed—in front of a fireplace almost as big as the picture windows in my condo. He was every inch the fallen aristocrat. Dressed in a suit that probably cost more than my car, a blue and white striped shirt with a white collar and a crimson tie. Tall and lean, with an impeccable posture that belied his age—he was seventy-eight. His silver hair was perfectly groomed and I was sure the pair of piercing blue eyes missed nothing.

I looked around the vast room. The word study did it little justice. It was a world from another time, a time when the robber barons ruled, a world of understated opulence and luxury. I was, on the one hand, impressed, and on the other, just a little sickened.

Family photos lined the walls. Photos of generations of Masons that seemed to stare down at their diminished heir.

"I was wondering when you'd get around to me," he began. "My father knew it was sabotage, you know?" he continued thoughtfully, swirling what I took to be a crystal glass of bourbon despite the early hour. "The fire department called it faulty wiring, but he found thermite residue. Military-grade accelerant." His eyes hardened, reflecting the bitterness. "The kind Rawlings Steel produced during the war."

"Did he take his findings to the authorities?" I asked, watching his face for signs of deception.

"With what proof? The evidence burned along with everything else." Mason's laugh was as bitter as his bourbon. "The

Rawlings had friends in high places back then. They still do. The investigation was closed before the ashes cooled."

Something caught my eye: fresh ash in the study's massive fireplace, despite the warm autumn afternoon. Moving closer under the pretense of admiring a portrait, I spotted fragments of a letterhead, the date still visible on charred embers: 1947.

"Lot of old papers being burned lately," I commented dryly, watching his reflection in the window.

Mason's expression didn't change, but his knuckles whitened around his glass. "Spring cleaning," he snapped. "Family business accumulates so much… unnecessary documentation accumulated over the years."

"Tell me about the night watchmen," I said, turning back to Mason. "The three men who died in that fire."

"A tragic accident." His response came too quickly. "They weren't supposed to be there that night."

"So I've heard," I said. "Someone changed the schedule."

The slightest flicker crossed his face. "It's all ancient history, Mr. Starke. Like this ridiculous feud with the Rawlings. Elizabeth should have left it all buried."

"Is that why she died?" I asked. "For digging up ancient history?"

Mason set his glass down carefully. "I think we're done here," he said.

And, as if on cue, two members of his security outfit appeared, both wearing Mason patches.

"One last question," I said. "What were you doing in the wine cellar ninety minutes before Elizabeth Rawlings collapsed?"

"Checking the wine, of course," he said. "Now, if you don't mind." He nodded to one of the guards and I was escorted out, politely and efficiently, to find Kate under similar guard waiting beside the car.

"Well, that was an experience," I said as I pulled the car door closed. "Did you have any luck?"

"If you can call it that," she replied. "I found multiple sets of recent tire tracks. Possibly Cadillacs and/or Range Rovers."

She opened the car door and slid into the passenger seat.

"Rawlings cars, d'you think?" I asked as I pulled my door shut. "A come to Jesus meeting with the supposed enemy?"

"Perhaps," she replied. "But there's more." She pulled up some photos on her phone. "I managed to get a glimpse through a window of their security office. It's quite an operation they have. They're wearing the same tactical gear we saw at the construction site, but the patches are different."

The pieces were falling into place. "What it appears we have here," I said, thoughtfully, "is a theatrical feud designed to mask cooperation between the two families, both of which are maintaining their own private security companies, companies that are working together while pretending to be rivals."

"That sounds awfully complicated," Kate replied, frowning. "Why would they do something like that?"

"Possibly as a diversion to hide... Geez, Kate, I don't know, but I sure as hell intend to find out."

My phone rang. It was Sarah Walker again. I frowned and answered it.

"Dad's remembered something about the fire he thinks you should know," she gabbled, "but he says I should only tell you in person. And Harry? Someone's watching his hospital room. Men in suits, trying to look inconspicuous."

"Go to the police department on Amnicola," I replied "and wait for us there. We're on our way. Don't talk to anyone."

As I drove away from the Mason estate, Kate reviewed our suspect list.

"I think we need to talk to everyone in both family inner circles," she said. "Starting with Elizabeth's immediate family."

"That makes sense," I replied. "James Rawlings Jr. is the obvious next step," I agreed. "And don't forget his wife, Eleanor."

Kate raised an eyebrow. "You think she's involved?" she asked.

"Probably not directly," I replied, "but she's been part of the family for over thirty years. She must know something."

"Or not," Kate argued. "Maybe they deliberately kept her in the dark."

"Either way, she's worth talking to," I said. "But she's not our highest priority right now."

Mentally, I added Eleanor's name to our growing list of interviews, though further down than the primary family members. In my experience, sometimes the most valuable perspectives came from those on the periphery.

We were halfway to the PD when Kate spotted the tail.

"We have a friend," she said. "A black SUV with tinted windows, three cars back."

I glanced up at the mirror. "Got it," I said.

"So both families are working together," Kate mused. "Using the feud as cover. But for what?"

"Something worth killing for," I replied, making a sudden right turn in an effort to lose our tail. "Something that started with the fire of '47," I said as I made a hard left.

Whoever was tailing us was pretty damn good. I couldn't lose them, and the SUV stayed with us until I pulled into the police department lot and parked facing the highway, and we watched as they drove slowly past. It was an arrogant warning. No doubt about it.

I left the car parked out front and we hurried into the lobby, where we found Sarah waiting for us. We escorted her to an interview room and sat her down with a cup of what I knew to be awful coffee.

"I'm going to record the interview, Sarah," I said, "for your security and mine." I nodded to the mirror and the red light on the camera turned on.

"Now," I said. "How's your father doing?"

"He's doing…" She paused, her eyes watering. "He's lying

there just thinking and thinking, going over his research in his mind. The doctor says his recovery... it's going to take a while."

I sat back in my chair. What she said didn't surprise me. Gunshot wounds are always devastating, and Dr. Walker was lucky to be alive.

"What did he tell you, Sarah?" I asked.

"The night watchmen," she said in a low voice. "They weren't just regular employees. Dad said he'd found their personnel files, and all three had worked for *both* families. He thinks they must have known something they shouldn't."

"I'm sure they did," I replied, "but what was it?"

"He thinks they knew what the mill was really producing during the war. He told me to tell you Elizabeth had proof that it wasn't just textiles, and the families were working together even then, using the mill to hide something. Something they're still hiding today."

My phone buzzed. I glanced at the screen. It was another text from my officers at the construction site. The workers had found something in the old mill foundations. Something metallic, with German writing.

I called the site and put the phone on speaker. The site foreman, Jim Stamford, answered.

"What's going on up there, Jim?" I asked.

"I dunno," he replied. "One of my workers found something. They must have had people watching the place because both families' security people are already here and they're shutting down the site. Something about unexploded war ordnance."

I looked at Sarah. She shook her head.

"Thanks, Jim," I said. "Keep me up to speed, will you?"

He said he would, and I disconnected the call.

"We need to get you back to your father," I said to Sarah.

But by the time we reached the hospital, Dr. Walker's room was empty. A nurse informed us that a representative of both families *and* Dr. Walker had signed the paperwork for his transfer to a private facility.

I was trying to find out what facility when Sarah's phone rang. It was her father's number. She answered it and put it on speaker.

"Your father's safe and in good hands," Margaret Mason said. "And he'll stay that way. We'll take good care of him, but we want his research files. All of them. We'll be in touch, Sarah." And she disconnected the call.

I locked eyes with Sarah, but only for a second before she looked away. "They kidnapped him," she muttered.

I felt bad for her. She had a choice to make: her father's life, or the truth about Chattanooga's most powerful families.

What she didn't know was that it was already too late for choices, and that Elizabeth Rawling's death had started something that couldn't be stopped. The fire that destroyed the mill in 1947 was about to ignite again, and would consume anyone and everyone who got too close to the truth.

"I need to go to my father's office," she whispered.

"Is that where your father keeps his files?" I asked.

She looked at me through hooded eyes. "Why d'you want to know?" she asked.

"They can't have them, Sarah," I replied. "You do know that, don't you?"

She heaved a sigh and nodded. "It's okay. They're safe in the university archive. He has a locker there. There's a key code to get into the archive and another to get into his locker. He made copies. They're in a file cabinet in his office. Those are what I'll give them."

I nodded and, without further argument, I told her I'd take her to her father's office. I also told her I wanted the codes, which she gave me, and then I took her, knowing the families would be watching.

Me? I couldn't help but wonder if we were doing the right

thing, playing their game. Before we left, however, I gave Kate the codes and told her to take a half-dozen uniformed officers and have them quietly move Dr. Walker's original research files to the police department and then for her to meet back up at his office.

The university was quiet for a Wednesday afternoon. *Too quiet*, I thought as I drove slowly through the campus, knowing the security cameras were tracking us, their red lights blinking like unspoken warnings.

"Tell me about the mill fire," I said as Sarah unlocked her father's office. "What exactly did your father find?"

She went to a file cabinet and pulled out a copy of an old blueprint, dated 1943, and laid it out on the table.

"The mill wasn't just a textile factory," she said. "See these modifications? Hidden sub-levels, reinforced storage areas, and this over here is a private rail spur. It's long gone now, of course." She pointed to additional notes. "All of it was funded jointly by the two families," she continued, "even though the mill supposedly belonged to the Masons."

It was at that moment that Kate arrived.

I looked at her. She nodded. I smiled at her.

"So, they were working together even as far back as 1943," Kate said, examining the plans.

Before Sarah could answer, I heard footsteps out in the hallway. A minute later, James Rawlings III appeared in the doorway, trying to look surprised at finding us there.

"Ms. Walker," he said smoothly. "I believe you have some files that belong to our families."

"Boy, do you have a nerve?" I said. "You kidnap her father and you walk in here like you own the place. I've a good mind to arrest you—"

"We did not kidnap Dr. Walker," he said, interrupting me. "He signed the transfer papers willingly, as the doctor and nurse witnessed. Now, the files, if you please?"

"You arrogant—" Kate discreetly squeezed my arm cutting me

off. I got the message. "How many people have died because of you and your families?" I asked. "I know of at least four, counting the three night watchmen. Those men died in the fire that supposedly started your family feud?"

Something flickered behind his slick facade, and he smiled. "Ancient history, Mr. Starke," he said, "is best left buried."

"Like when Elizabeth tried to expose you?" Kate asked.

"The files?" he said.

Sarah pushed the stack of files across the table to him.

"The map, too, if you please."

Sarah folded it and placed it on top of the files.

James was about to pick them up when his phone buzzed. He read the message. His face tightened. He looked up at Sarah and said, "Ms. Walker, your father is asking for you. There's a car waiting outside."

"She's not going anywhere," I said.

"Actually," Sarah said, "I am." She gave me a meaningful look. "My father needs me."

We watched her leave with James, knowing the families would find only the copies of Dr. Walker's research in the files. The originals, the evidence, was already safe deep inside the police department. And I couldn't help but wonder what their reaction would be.

"They're getting sloppy," Kate said after they'd gone. "All this overt pressure. They're running scared."

My phone lit up with a message from an unknown number: a set of coordinates followed by a single word and a time: "Tonight. 9pm."

I had Kate try to track its origin, but to no avail. Whoever the sender was, they were smart enough to use a burner phone.

The location mapped to an old warehouse near the river, one of the few buildings that had survived the urban renewal. Property records showed it had passed back and forth between the families for decades, each transfer marked by public disputes that had made headlines.

"More performances," Kate said, checking the address. "Making sure everyone saw them fighting over it."

"While they used it together," I added. "Like everything else."

Kate and I started our surveillance of the warehouse early that evening, from a distance. Right on schedule, they arrived: an SUV and two two-ton unmarked trucks into which they loaded fourteen large wooden crates.

"Same operation, different generation," Kate murmured as she photographed the license plates. "What are we going to do about it?"

"There's not much we can do," I replied. "It could be a legitimate business operation. We have no probable cause."

I didn't like it, but it was true. Was it worth taking a risk? At that point in the investigation, no. So we continued to watch until, only twenty minutes later, they closed the trucks' tailgates and the little convoy drove away.

I was just about to go to the car and follow them when my phone buzzed. It was Sarah Walker. She'd gotten away from her handlers long enough to send a message: "Dad's safe. But I heard them talking. They found something in the mill foundations and they're moving it, tonight."

IT WAS ALMOST TOTALLY dark when we approached the construction site. The same security teams we'd seen at the warehouse were already there, inside the exposed mill foundations.

"Look at their gear," Kate whispered as we watched from behind a stack of concrete blocks. "Those are the same teams that shot at Walker."

I nodded, put my night-vision binoculars to my eyes and watched them retrieving... something from the foundations:

metal containers, similar to the box Walker found before he was shot.

My phone vibrated. It was another text from Sarah. "Dad says to check the west wall. There's a hidden sub-basement. He says Elizabeth found it. It's where they stored the German shipments."

But before we could move, headlights swept across the site as a Bentley and a Mercedes arrived together. A moment later, Thomas Mason and James Rawlings Jr., the family patriarchs themselves, exited the vehicles together. They'd obviously come to oversee the operation.

"The fire didn't destroy everything," Mason's voice carried clearly through the night.

"Elizabeth found the manifests," Rawlings replied. "She was going to expose us, all of us."

"We're exposed anyway," Mason replied. "Walker's research…"

"…will disappear like everything else that threatens us," Rawlings finished for him.

Watching them work together to preserve their secrets, it was hard to believe anyone had ever thought their feud was real.

A moment later, a man I took to be a member of one of the security teams emerged from the foundations carrying a metal box. Even at a distance, through my night vision glasses, I could make out the faded Nazi stamps on its side.

"Harry," Kate whispered urgently. "Look at their gear. Those aren't private security patches. Those are federal badges."

I searched the site with my binoculars. She was right. The family security teams were gone. What we'd thought was going to be a family cleanup operation had turned into a federal raid. The families had led them right to the evidence, but why?

I focused again on the two patriarchs. They were already in handcuffs as floodlights illuminated the site. More federal agents emerged from hiding places.

"She did it, damn her," Thomas Mason said as they led him

past our position. "That bitch Elizabeth finally brought it all down."

Nope, I thought. *Something's not right. It feels... wrong.* The patriarchs had surrendered too easily. Their security teams had disappeared too quickly.

"So the feud was fake," Kate said, watching federal crews document evidence. "Right from the beginning, But why maintain it for so long? What were they really hiding?"

The answer to that question would cost more lives before we found it. But for now, as we watched the patriarchs being driven away, we thought we'd seen the end of the story.

We were wrong. The fire that started in 1947 was still burning.

CAMERON HILL'S SECRETS
Morning, October 18

IT HAD BEEN A LONG DAY, so Kate stayed over again that night and, tired as we were, we were in bed and asleep by ten-thirty.

As usual, I rose early the following morning, Thursday, and went for a six-mile run along Lake Resort Drive.

I returned almost an hour later to find Kate wearing one of my T-shirts and little else, making breakfast of scrambled eggs, sausage and bacon. *Nice,* I thought as I headed for the shower.

Fifteen minutes later, feeling refreshed and ready for the day, I was back in the kitchen, where Kate was sitting at the table, a cup of coffee in hand.

"Feel better now?" she asked over the rim of her cup.

"I do," I replied, as I poured myself some coffee, took my breakfast from the warm oven, sat down opposite her and stared at her.

"What?" she asked, frowning.

"Nothing," I replied. "Well, I was just thinking how nice this is, you and me, eating an early breakfast together. Very domesticated."

"Don't get used to it," she said, dryly, and got up to pour herself more coffee.

"You didn't check in with the chief last night," she said without looking round. "You'd better do it this morning."

"What am I going to tell him?" I asked. "We still don't know who killed Elizabeth. And I have a gut feeling all is not as it seems. Those two gave in far too easily, don't you think? Something smells."

Kate nodded thoughtfully, then said, "Changing the subject; what was in those metal boxes, I wonder? Some of them had what looked like Nazi markings on them. I guess we'll never know now the feds have them."

"Yeah…" I began, then thought for a moment before continuing, "How the hell did that happen? And how the hell did the feds become involved? It all seemed a little too… staged, didn't it?"

Kate nodded. "I'd like to know more about the connections between the families and their properties. I think we need to visit the city records office. That would be the logical place to find the historical Cameron Hill documents to the properties there, and the old mill."

"Yep, that makes sense," I replied. "Give me a minute to report to the chief and we'll go."

I looked at my watch. It was almost eight-thirty, and so, with a sigh, I tapped in his number. He answered on the first ring.

"Starke," he snapped. "I thought we agreed you'd report in daily before five-thirty. What happened?"

I bared my teeth, took a deep breath, then dove right in, "Well, it's like this, Chief…" and I proceeded to fill him in with the events of the previous day and evening. When I'd finished my long diatribe, he raised the inevitable question: who killed Elizabeth Rawlings? And I had to admit to him I was no closer to the answer than I was three days ago. "But I'm working on it," I told him.

He ended call the with a stern admonition that I was to check in as agreed and to get my butt out of my hands and bring the investigation to a satisfactory resolution, and quickly. Again, I told him I was working on it.

Was I bothered? No. I'd gone through it so many times before, so I was used to it. I hung up and smiled to myself. I turned and looked at Kate who was, by then, on her third cup of coffee, and said, "Shall we go?"

THE MASSIVE LEATHER-BOUND books in the city archives told a story of power, wealth, and careful planning. The old black and white photographs were impressive. Before urban renewal had razed the neighborhood, the Rawlings and Mason mansions had stood side by side, overlooking the river like twin thrones.

"Look at this," Kate said, spreading out a map from 1945 on the table in front of me. I looked at it in silence. The yellowed document showed the elaborate layout of both properties. "Private driveways, shared gardens, even a joint gatehouse. The two families weren't just neighbors, they were practically one single household."

"Until they weren't," I said.

A different set of records painted a modern picture: shell companies with Delaware addresses and offshore accounts, all tracing back to Elizabeth Rawlings. Over the past year, she'd been quietly acquiring a massive parcel of North Shore property. The development plans in her portfolio would have completely transformed the waterfront and had apparently gotten her killed.

I looked at my watch. It was just after eleven and I was... I dunno, bored; I suppose. So, I sucked in a deep breath, took Kate by the hand and said, "I'm done. I can't stand anymore of this..." I waved my hand over the cluttered table, then said, "Let's wrap this up and get out of here."

We were on our way out of the building when my phone buzzed. It was Sarah Walker.

"They're moving him again," she said. "But he managed to tell me where to find the property records from the old mansions. He said to give them to you. There's a connection to the mill fire."

"Can you bring them?"

"I'm already on my way to the police department," she replied. "But Harry, I'm being followed."

I gave her an alternate address, a coffee shop in the Bluff View Art District overlooking the river.

As Kate and I waited, I thought about Dr. Walker's last words before being taken: 'The foundations were just a distraction.' But for the life of me I couldn't figure out what he meant.

Sarah arrived about ten minutes after we did. She looked exhausted, and scared, constantly glancing over her shoulder. She pulled a stack of aged documents from her shoulder bag and sat down.

"These were hidden in Dad's library," she said, spreading them across the table. "Purchase agreements, construction plans, and this..." She opened a faded blueprint showing a tunnel system beneath both mansions that connected to the old mill.

"Maintenance tunnels?" Kate asked.

Sarah shook her head. "No. If you look at the reinforcement specifications, you'll see they weren't built for sewage or steam pipes. They were designed to move stuff to and from the mill and the river."

"Like gold bars with German stamps," I said, thinking of the containers from the mill foundations.

A handwritten note in the blueprint's margin caught my eye: "Connection to M facility complete. Ready for contingency plan."

"Any idea what that means?" I asked.

"M facility," Sarah said. "Dad thinks it's a reference to the Mason textile mill, and that the tunnels were their escape route. When the federal investigation started getting close in '47, they burned the mill to hide the evidence, but saved what they could by taking it out through the tunnels."

"And Elizabeth found these plans?" Kate asked.

"Not just found them," Sarah replied. "She also realized some of the tunnels are still active and connect to the Chattanooga Underground."

I looked at Kate. She nodded. She knew all about the city beneath the city, as did I.

"Her development project would have exposed them," Sarah continued. "Look at these ground-penetrating radar scans from the development site. These are the tunnels. The network is mostly intact."

My phone lit up. It was James Rawlings III requesting an urgent meeting. I ignored it. A minute later, Kate received a similar text from Margaret Mason. Both wanted to meet at the same location, the old River Street warehouse.

"They're not even trying to hide their cooperation anymore," Kate noted.

"Because they're running out of time," Sarah said. "We think, my dad and me, that they're still moving… things, stuff, whatever, out through the old tunnel system…"

She trailed off as a black SUV pulled up outside the coffee shop. Through the window, I recognized the driver. He was a member of the federal team that raided the mill site the night before, only now he was wearing Mason patches instead of federal badges.

What the hell? I thought.

"Back door," I told Sarah, but she was already moving.

We slipped out after her and got her safely away to Kate's apartment in East Brainerd. But, as we drove, I couldn't help but think that something about the families' sudden openness, about their mutual cooperation, was bothering me. It felt... wrong, somehow. They were showing their hand too easily.

5

WE SPENT the rest of the morning reviewing the mansion records in Kate's living room. The documents told a story at odds with Chattanooga's accepted history. The Rawlings and Mason families hadn't just been neighbors, they'd built their Cameron Hill mansions together, designing them as two halves of a single operation.

"These construction costs," Kate said, examining the figures. "They're way too high for the early 1900s, even for mansions this size."

"Look at the materials list," Sarah added. "They weren't building homes, they were building infrastructure."

I had no answer to it. All I could do was stare at the blueprints and wonder what the hell it was all about. In the end, I got up and walked away into the kitchen and sat down at the table to think. I hadn't been there but a minute when my phone buzzed. I looked at the screen. I recognized the number. Mabel Henderson was returning my call.

Mabel was someone I'd known for most of my life. She'd known my mother, and she still talked to my father. At ninety-two, she was a spry old bird and one of the few people still alive who remembered Cameron Hill before urban renewal. Her father had been a gardener for both families. I'd called her earlier and left a message explaining that I was looking into the two families, and would she give me a few moments of her time?

We left Sarah at Kate's apartment and went to her assisted living home overlooking the river.

"Mabel," I said when we walked into her room. "How the hell are you?"

"Oh, Harry, it's you. How nice to see you... Uh oh! Who's your friend?" Despite her age, her mind was sharp as clear crystal.

"You don't change, do you, Mabel?" I said. "This is Kate, my partner."

She squinted up at her from her recliner. "Well, step forward, young woman, so I can see you. These old eyes don't work like they used to."

Kate took a step forward, smiling.

"Hmm," Mabel said, then looked at me, then back at Kate, and nodded. "Partner, you say. What exactly does that mean, Harry?"

"Whatever you want it to, Mabel," I replied. "We work together and—"

"Sleep together," she finished for me. "How long have you two been an item?"

"That's enough, Mabel," I said. "We're here to talk about the Rawlings and the Masons, remember?"

"Cheeky boy," she said. "Of course I remember. Well, sit your-selves down. What d'you want to know?"

"What do you remember of them?" I asked as we sat down.

"Humm..." She thought for a moment, then said, "Rich, arrogant, self-important, typical of the wealthy class, but you know all that."

"Tell me about the feud," I said.

"Oh, that old thing," she said with a smile. "It began the night after the fire of '47… Or was it the day after that? It was, so my father said, something to do with the ownership of the old mill. I believe it belonged to the Masons. But the business? Ownership of that was always a little murky."

"What exactly was the business?" Kate asked.

"Well now, that's the big question, isn't it?" she replied. "Textiles was the official tale." She looked at me, then at Kate. "Sorry, but apart from a few whispered rumors, I've heard nothing to the contrary."

"Your father was the gardener for the two families, wasn't he?" I asked.

She nodded. "He was."

"Look, Mabel, what I'm trying to do here is find out who killed Elizabeth Rawlings. I need to know what was going on up there on Cameron Hill, before the redevelopment."

She nodded. "I know what you're after, Harry. Let an old lady have her day, will you?" She sat back in her recliner and sighed.

"Both mansions were demolished in 1952 as part of the West Side Urban Renewal project and, as you know, that's all just been demolished to make room for that fancy new office building everyone's raving about."

"And the mill?" Kate asked.

At that, Mabel pulled a face, then said, "All I know is that it burned to the ground in 1947. The foundations are still there, I believe."

"And the tunnels?" Kate asked. "There are two shown on an old blueprint."

"Oh, those tunnels," she said, eyes bright with memory. "Blueprints, you say? I doubt they're accurate. Nothing about those families is. My father said they ran throughout Cameron Hill.

The families used them during Prohibition, you know. But in '47…" She leaned forward, lowering her voice. "The night of the fire… trucks came and went for hours. He saw men carrying out something heavy. Gold, some folks said. Others said weapons."

"Did the police investigate?" I asked.

Mabel laughed. "Police? Hah!" she sat back in her chair and closed her eyes. "Back then," she continued, "the families owned the police. Whatever went through those tunnels stayed secret. But Elizabeth…" She smiled sadly. "She came here last month asking questions. She said it was time for the truth."

"Did she find it?" Kate asked.

"She must have," Mabel replied. "Otherwise, why would they kill her—?"

It was at that moment that a nurse came in and interrupted her, saying she needed to rest. And I had to admit, the old girl looked a bit peaky. So I nodded to Kate and stood up.

"Mable," I said. "I think we've taken up enough of your time, but I'll come back and see you soon." And I turned to leave.

We were at the door when she called after us, "Check the old boathouse. The one they pretended to fight over in '48. That fight was another family fake like all the rest."

"So, what d'you think?" I asked as we walked back to the car.

"I think we know nothing more than we did," Kate said. "She's a lovely old lady, though. I can see why you like her."

"Yes, I like her. I like her a lot. They don't make 'em like her anymore. It will be a sad day for me when she's gone. But what she said about the boathouse. It would be the one just to the left of the public boat ramp, wouldn't it?"

By then, we were back at the car.

"Yes, I think so," Kate said, as she opened the passenger side door and climbed in. "I saw it somewhere that the Rawlings and Masons were feuding over it. They even went to court over it."

"Yes, here it is," she said a moment later after pulling up the records of the dispute. "Look at this from 1948," she said, turning the laptop toward me so I could see it. There was a photo and an article that showed both families in court, battling over a seemingly worthless piece of riverfront property.

"And look at this," she said after finding a survey map. "The boathouse sits directly above where the tunnel system meets the river. Do the tunnels connect with the Underground, d'you think?"

I glanced sideways at her laptop, then returned my attention to the road and said, "I don't know about that, but it would have been the perfect place to load and unload without drawing attention, and their public fight over the property would have kept everyone else away from the area."

"True," Kate said, "but the boathouse wasn't the only property they fought over. There were others, some of them downtown—which again makes me wonder if they were somehow using the Underground. I mean, almost every public dispute seems to be centered on locations connected to the tunnel network."

"Can you get that for me?" I said as my phone lit up.

She tapped my phone in its holder, looked at it and said, "It's another message from James Rawlings III. This time he's says he has proof that the Mason family was responsible for Elizabeth Rawlings' death—damn!" she muttered as her own phone chirped.

"Same thing," she said, "only mine's from Margaret Mason. She's claiming she has evidence the Rawlings family killed Elizabeth.

"Still playing their roles," I said. "Even now. Ignore it."

I glanced at the dashboard clock. It was just after four o'clock.

"We need to go back to your apartment and talk to Sarah," I said. "We need to find out exactly what her father found."

6

SARAH WALKER
Evening, October 18, 4:00pm

"What d'you have, Sarah?" I asked, as we walked into Kate's apartment, too tired for small talk. The long days were beginning to get to me.

"I haven't had time to go through it all," Sarah replied. "At this point, I really only know what he told me. And that was that he'd found proof that both families worked together to kill Elizabeth. Just like they worked together to set the mill fire. But look, if we go through this together," she waved a hand over the papers she'd spread out over the kitchen table, "it will maybe go a little faster... don't you think?"

I nodded and said, "Let's get to it, then. Where do we start?"

As the afternoon turned into evening, we followed Sarah's father's research trail, Kate photographing everything: papers, blueprints, photographs, sending it all to the cloud and her laptop.

Dr. Walker had methodically documented how the families had used their theatrical feud to maintain control of key properties across Chattanooga, each public battle carefully choreographed to hide their true family cooperation. The depth of it was mind-blowing.

At five o'clock, I reluctantly made my report to the chief, purposely neglecting to mention Sarah Walker's involvement, and then listened to his predictable admonition that he needed a result, and soon.

By six o'clock I'd had enough. My eyes were hurting and my head was aching. "D'you have anything to eat in that refrigerator?" I asked, gazing at it.

"Some left over pizza, is all," she replied.

"Better than nothing," I said, grudgingly.

She smiled, went to the fridge, took out what was left of an extra-large mushroom and pepperoni, and stuck it in the microwave. It turned out there was enough for two slices apiece. Nice!

"I've had it with all this research," I said as I washed my last bite down with a gulp of coffee. "Mabel mentioned the boathouse. I think we should take a look at it. You want to join us, Sarah, or d'you want to stay here and do more of... this?" I nodded at the stack of paperwork.

"I need a break, too," she replied. "I'll come with you, but... I'd like to freshen up a little first."

She looked at Kate. Kate smiled, then said, "You know where the bathroom is but..." she looked her up and down, "I have plenty of tops and T's that might fit you, but I think everything else will be too big, or should I say long, for you."

"A quick wash and fresh T-shirt will be fine," she replied, smiling. "And thank you."

"Umm, d'you mind moving this along a little," I said. "I was hoping for an early night. It's almost six-thirty."

Chapter 6

IT WAS after seven-thirty when we parked near the old boathouse, now abandoned and officially condemned.

We exited the car and cautiously made our way down to the riverbank, staying out of sight behind the natural growth: shrubs, bushes and trees. The Riverwalk had not yet reached that section of Ross's Landing.

The structure leaned over the Tennessee River like a drunken man about to fall, its weathered boards glowing faintly in the waxing moonlight.

"I wonder if there's any security," Kate said. "Maybe we should call for backup."

"It looks quiet enough," I said.

"Yeah, well," Kate muttered. "We all know how that can go."

Sarah studied the building through a pair of binoculars Kate had loaned her. "There's power to it. I can see the meter - it's spinning."

We went closer. She was right. The supposedly condemned boat house was using enough electricity to run a small warehouse.

I paused for a moment, turned and looked up at Cameron Hill behind me. The earthmoving machinery, silhouetted against the moonlit sky, was silent.

"Elizabeth's development plans," Sarah whispered, checking her father's notes. "They would have dug right through this section into the tunnel system. No wonder they tried to stop it. Whatever it is they're still moving through here would have been exposed."

"It still will, if I have my way," I said. "We need to get closer. There's something going on in there and I want to know what it is."

By then we were close, on a foliage-covered mound, looking down at the structure, when we heard a boat approaching, running dark. They cut the engine, and it slowly drifted up to the boathouse dock.

We watched as two men jumped off onto the dock—leaving two in the boat—and began unloading crates into the boathouse.

"Those containers," Kate said. "They look the same as the ones we saw at the mill site."

My phone vibrated. I glanced at it. It was a text from Mabel Henderson's nurse. *Mr. Starke. Mabel is not doing well. She has something she wants to tell you. She says she wants to talk to you about something she was too scared to mention before. Can you come?*

But before I could answer the text, headlights swept over the area. Multiple vehicles were approaching.

As it happened, we were within earshot of the boathouse, watching as a large black SUV followed by two smaller ones pulled up in front of the building. There was a moment of silence, and then James Rawlings III and Margaret Mason stepped down out of the SUV and approached the front doors. Six armed security guards who'd exited the two smaller vehicles followed them at a respectful distance.

"The tunnels have to be cleared tonight," I heard Rawlings say as he turned and looked up at the silhouettes on Cameron Hill.

He was quiet for a moment, rubbing his chin with his hand, then said, "The development project starts preliminary drilling tomorrow."

"That old bitch Elizabeth," Margaret snarled. "Even in death, she's still causing problems."

They entered the boathouse together, followed by the security guards, if that's what they were. Their uniforms all showed the same patches with an insignia we hadn't seen before.

"That symbol," Sarah said, zooming in with her camera. "It's in Dad's research."

"Whatever it is, they're moving it through the tunnels," Kate said. "And they're in a hurry to clear it out."

"The manifests my father found," Sarah said as we watched from our vantage point. "Recent ones, using the same coding system they used back in the '40s. He said Elizabeth discovered they'd never stopped running shipments through the tunnels. They just updated their methods."

"We need to call for backup," I said.

Kate's scanner crackled. Fish and Wildlife agents were reporting unusual activity on the river. Multiple boats running fast without lights.

"Call for backup," I said. "Do it now... No, wait. Look. Something's happening." I pointed to the boathouse. James and Margaret had emerged, their faces illuminated by their phone screens. They looked worried.

"There must have been a leak," I heard James say. "They're moving in tomorrow morning. Someone must have talked."

But Margaret wasn't listening. She was already ordering the security team into action. "Clear everything out. Use the old contingency routes."

"Like in '47," James added. "When they burned the mill."

"Idiot!" Margaret snapped.

The activity below kicked into high gear. Two more boats appeared, both running dark. By then, the security team had disappeared inside the boathouse.

My phone buzzed. It was another text from Mabel Henderson's nurse. *I'm sorry to tell you, Mabel passed away twenty-minutes ago. She asked me to tell you about a hidden room beneath the boathouse. And she said something about records the families had stored there. That's it. That's all she said. Please pray for her.*

"Damn," I whispered. "Mabel passed away... They're not just clearing out the product, whatever it is, they're clearing out the evidence."

Another vehicle pulled up, a Cadillac. Thomas Mason emerged, followed by James Rawlings Jr.

Geez, I thought, *the patriarchs have come to oversee the operation personally.*

"Elizabeth's development plans," old man Mason said to his

daughter. "She designed them specifically to expose the tunnel system."

"She knew we'd have to clear everything out," Rawlings Jr. added. "The old bitch knew we'd get sloppy under pressure."

"Like now," Mason agreed. "We're exposed. Too many people asking questions. That Walker girl and her father…"

"They will be handled," Rawlings finished. "As was Elizabeth."

Sarah's hands tightened on her binoculars at the casual mention of her father. Below us, the clean-up operation continued. The boats began to leave, heading downriver toward Nickajack Lake, running dark.

"Geez," I snapped. "Where's that backup?"

"You told me to wait, remember?" Kate said.

I closed my eyes. *Holy cow,* I thought. *There will be holy hell to pay when the chief finds out.*

"Hey," Kate whispered. "Look!"

I looked. The security team was bringing out dozens of banker's boxes and loading them into the SUVs and the trunk of the Cadillac.

I called for backup, but before I could finish the call, a series of explosions lit up the night. The ground beneath our feet trembled, then shook. They were collapsing the tunnels as they retreated, destroying the evidence they couldn't move.

My phone vibrated. It was becoming a very busy night.

It was a text from Dr. Walker. Where the hell he was we didn't know, but he'd obviously found a sympathetic someone to get a message out. *The development plans. Elizabeth hid something in the original blueprints. A message of some sort about the boathouse records.*

Before I could respond, the night was lit up by what appeared to be dozens of flashing blue and white lights as several more vehicles pulled up. The feds had arrived. Real ones this time. I recognized some of them from previous investigations.

"That's a bummer for them," Kate said. "The families weren't expecting them until morning."

The scene below erupted into chaos. The security team scattered. The two boats at the dock disappeared into the darkness at high speed, and the patriarchs were quickly whisked away along with the records, all except for a single filing cabinet, tipped over on its side, its drawers out, papers scattered everywhere.

And, for some reason, James and Margaret were also left behind along with their security team, which quickly reassembled into something resembling professional order.

Me? I had a deep feeling that something about what had just happened was off. Why did they take the old men and leave James and Margaret, the filing cabinet and the security people behind? It made no sense.

"Those feds," I said. "There's something going on. Something's not right. Why did they leave them behind... and the cabinet?"

"The cabinet," Sarah whispered. "They left it because there's nothing of importance in it. It's another distraction."

I felt the earth move beneath my feet. It felt like a mini earthquake. The last of the tunnels were collapsing.

My backup finally arrived, too late to be of any use.

James and Margaret left a few minutes after the patriarchs were taken away, leaving behind their security team with orders to make sure the clean-up was completed.

Barely had they left when another SUV and a large black van arrived and disgorged what looked to me to be a half-dozen FBI agents and a CSI team. They were, of course, too late, but, so I learned later, by dawn they had secured the boathouse and completely cleaned it out. The filing cabinet? Again, so I learned later, told a carefully curated story. It contained just enough evidence to suggest a small-scale smuggling operation run by the two junior members of the feuding families, but nothing that hinted at the true scope of the families' cooperation.

"Elizabeth must have known something like this would happen," Sarah said as we watched from our overlook. "Which is why she embedded the evidence in her development plans. The plans themselves are the message."

By then, Kate was sitting on her haunches with her laptop open on her knees, staring at a blueprint. "Look at these elevation markers. They don't match standard survey data."

"They're coordinates, I think," Sarah replied. "My dad said Elizabeth was brilliant with codes. And that he thinks she used the development plans to map the entire tunnel network - past and present."

My phone lit up again with another text from Dr. Walker. *Elizabeth had a safe in her office.*

Yeah, I thought. "And somewhere downstream," I said, "decades of evidence is disappearing while the federal agents catalog the scraps the families left behind."

"They'll find enough to make some arrests," Kate said. "Minor charges, and they'll dismiss them just as they always have whenever someone got close."

"But Elizabeth left us a map," Sarah said. "And they don't know we have it."

The light of the moon, now high overhead, revealed fresh scars in the earth where the tunnels below had collapsed. *Three generations of secrets buried forever*, I thought, *while two of Chattanooga's most distinguished families get away with murder, literally.*

But something had changed. The families' carefully constructed choreography was showing cracks. In their haste to clear the tunnels, they'd exposed the scale of their operation. Their perfect performance was finally faltering.

"Elizabeth Rawlings was one smart lady," I said. "I think she knew something like this would happen, planned for it, even."

I watched as the feds photographed the empty boathouse. "I think she designed her development project to force exactly this result."

I shook my head and smiled to myself. As Margaret said, even in death, the old girl was still pushing the families toward exposure. The question was: how many more would have to die before the truth finally emerged?

The moon climbed higher as we crept away from our vantage point. I took one last look and again I had to smile. Elizabeth's death had lit a fuse that was still burning, and no amount of collapsed tunnels or theatrical feuding could stop what was coming.

BURIED LIES

Friday Morning, October 19

It was almost midnight when we arrived back at my apartment. We were all bushed. Sarah was so tired she could barely walk.

We all had cornflakes and then went to bed. Sarah in the spare room and Kate and I… well, you get the picture, I'm sure. It was twelve-fifty-five when Kate turned off the light.

Tired as we all were, I'd set my phone alarm for six-thirty.

I woke to the sound of drums five and a half hours later, feeling as if I'd been dragged through the bushes backward, which, in a way, I suppose I had.

Kate and I had been an item for slightly more than three years. We weren't living together, but she kept several changes of clothes at my condo, so getting showered and dressed in clean, fresh clothes was never a problem.

As I went downstairs to make coffee, I heard the sound of running water in the spare bathroom, which told me that Sarah was already up, too. Whether or not that was a good thing, I wasn't sure. I liked my alone time with Kate.

Usually, I would go for an early morning run, sometimes with Kate, but mostly on my own. That morning, however, I elected to stay home and make breakfast. The plan was that Kate, Sarah and I would go to Elizabeth Rawlings' home and find the safe Sarah's father had said we'd find in her office.

It was a little after ten that morning when James Rawlings III reluctantly let us into the mansion and led us to Elizabeth's study.

It took us more than an hour to find the safe, and less than five minutes for Kate to open it. It was hidden low down behind the walnut wall paneling to the left of the window, the morning sun filtering through the heavy curtains.

Kate and I knelt before the safe and I watched as she did her thing with the combination, while Sarah Walker sat at Elizabeth's desk and consulted her father's notes.

James Rawlings III, who'd insisted on being there, hovered nearby, radiating nervous energy. And I didn't blame him for that after last night's performance at the boathouse, which, of course, we didn't mention.

The safe swung open with a well-oiled whisper, to reveal stacks of documents that smelled of age and, I hoped, secrets. A leather-bound diary sat on top, its pages brittle with age. The first page displayed "Emma Rawlings, 1947" in faded ink.

"That's my great-grandmother's diary," James said, his voice tight. "Grandmother Elizabeth found it last month."

The diary's first entry set the tone: *What we're doing is necessary, but God help us if anyone ever discovers the truth. The Mason collaboration must remain hidden, no matter the cost.*

"Can I see?" Sarah asked.

I nodded and handed it to her, much to James' consternation.

She flipped through the pages, speed reading as she went, then, more than halfway through, she stopped flipping and said, "Both families were already working together in 1947, and they had been long before the mill fire."

Kate, who was methodically photographing documents, said, "Look at these shipping manifests. German companies, Swiss bank transfers, gold shipments disguised as textile machinery."

The safe contained three generations of carefully preserved evidence. Property deeds showing joint ownerships hidden behind shell companies. Financial records documenting shared accounts. Security reports from the tunnel system's early operations.

"Elizabeth didn't just find proof of past crimes," I said, studying a recent bank statement. "She found evidence the operation never stopped. Why was she not a part of it all, I wonder?"

James cleared his throat nervously. "There's something else you should see." He took a small plastic bag from his jacket pocket and held it up. I could see it contained a charred piece of fabric. The Mason mill's logo was still visible on the unburned section. "From last night," he said. "Someone left this after…"

His voice trailed off as a security alert chimed on his phone. He took it out, looked at it, then at me, and said, "It's Mason's security people." He checked the feed. "But they're not supposed to…" His eyes widened. "They're not here for show."

Kate was already moving. "Get the diary and the recent files and leave the rest," she snapped.

"No," Sarah interrupted. "They'll destroy everything. My father's reputation, Elizabeth's evidence. It will all disappear."

She was right. We could hear several vehicles moving around the house. This wasn't another performance. This was the real thing.

"Kate, call for backup," I said.

The security team hit all four entrances simultaneously.

"Panic room," James said, leading us toward a hidden door. "Behind the bookcase. Now!"

We barely made it inside and closed the door before they breached the study. Through the one-way glass panel, we watched them methodically sweep the room.

Kate took out her phone. "Dispatch, this is Sergeant Gazzara," she said, keeping her voice low. "Request immediate assistance at the Rawlings estate. Multiple armed suspects, potential hostage situation." And she gave the address and our location within the house.

"ETA fifteen minutes," came the response. "All available units responding."

"They're not even pretending anymore," Kate whispered, filming everything with her Nikon Coolpix.

Sarah clutched the diary to her chest as we watched and listened to them tear the study apart. The safe stood open, but fortunately, most of its contents were already in Kate's camera and Sarah's bag.

James was watching the security teams with growing unease. "This isn't right. They're not following protocol. This is like…"

"Like Elizabeth's murder," I finished for him. "No more theater. Just threat elimination."

The teams were placing charges now—what looked to me like small military devices designed to start a controlled burn. They were going to destroy the study and everything in it.

"There's a tunnel access point," James whispered. "Here in the panic room. It connects to the old network."

"The network they just collapsed?" Kate asked.

"No, not all of it," he replied. "Some sections were too valuable to destroy, like this one."

Through the glass, we watched Margaret Mason enter the study. She surveyed the scene with cold efficiency, then spoke into a radio: "Finish it. Then find them."

Hours later, we learned the responding units had found the

house secured by Mason's private security people, claiming to be conducting a "training exercise" with the family's permission and that the fire was accidental and quickly contained. By the time officers gained entry, Elizabeth's study was already destroyed, and we were long gone through the tunnel system.

"They switched to cleanup mode as soon as they heard sirens," Kate said. "Standard procedure, I suppose. When official law enforcement arrives, they immediately transition to their cover story."

"And with their connections, they managed to stall them long enough to destroy the evidence," I added. "But they didn't get everything, did they, Sarah?"

Sarah shook her head. "The most important pieces are still safe."

The air in the tunnel was thick with dust as we followed James through the darkness.

"The families maintained key sections," James explained as we moved deeper into the network.

"Look at this," Kate said, pointing to fresh tire tracks in the tunnel dust. "Recent traffic."

"Here," James said, stopping at a modern security door. "This section connects to the old Mason property."

He tapped a code into the door's electronic keypad. The lock clicked. He pushed the door open, and we stepped inside a climate-controlled storage room filled with filing cabinets.

"This must be their archives," Kate said as she examined the setup. "Looks like everything they couldn't risk storing above ground they stored down here."

Sarah, cross-referencing the diary with her father's notes, muttered, "The coding system: it's based on the development plans. Elizabeth used the same cipher in reverse. From what I can tell, she wasn't just planning construction, she was mapping their entire operation and, I think from what I'm reading here, that the feud was Emma Rawlings' idea."

But before we could process this, I heard voices echoing in the tunnel. Someone was coming and coming fast.

"We have to go," James said, moving to a far wall. "This way but…" He hesitated. "It leads to the Mason estate."

"We have no choice," I said. "Let's hope they're not expecting us."

The passage to the Mason estate appeared to be quite new.

"What about the security cameras?" I asked.

"I turned them off as soon as we entered the archive," James replied, "but it won't be long before they figure it out," he said, hurrying us along. "The system logs everything."

Sarah had stopped suddenly, staring at a page in the diary. "Wait," she said. "This entry from September 17, 1947 - the day after the mill fire. It's not coded like the others."

She read aloud: "The gold is secure. New shipments arriving weekly through river route. Thomas and Richard have expanded operations beyond original scope. God forgive us all for what we've done." She paused, then said, "What did she mean, what we've done?"

"The night watchmen," I said. "They discovered something they weren't supposed to see."

James nodded grimly. "They found evidence of the German connections. The families couldn't risk exposure."

"So they burned the mill," I added. "Killed the witnesses. Started the public feud as cover."

The ground beneath our feet shook, and dust rained down from the roof of the tunnel.

"What the hell was that?" Kate asked.

"I'd say they just destroyed the archive," I said. "Come on. Let's get out of here."

And we hurried on along the tunnel until we finally emerged into a wine cellar beneath the Mason estate.

"Hang on a minute," Sarah said as James rushed to the door. "I think there's something here, in this cellar. The diary mentions a hidden vault behind the wine racks. Apparently, Elizabeth found it last month."

James looked surprised. "That's impossible. Even I didn't know about…"

He trailed off as Sarah located the hidden mechanism. A section of the wall slid aside, revealing a modern security door.

"She even noted the code," Sarah said as she tapped it in.

The vault door opened silently, revealing a small room containing two modern computer servers humming alongside several more filing cabinets and two banks of safety deposit boxes, each bearing both family crests.

"I guess this is where they keep everything too sensitive for regular storage," James said.

Kate moved methodically through the room, photographing everything. "These shipping manifests are recent," she said. "And these security protocols, personnel files… Harry, they're still running the same operations they started during the war."

"But modernized and expanded," I added, examining a ledger. "They're now into art theft, antiquities, money laundering, and God only knows what else."

"Shush!" Kate said. "Listen… Geez, someone's coming, a lot of someones."

She was right. I could hear running footsteps echoing above us.

"There's no way out," I said, looking around.

"Yes, there is," James said. "There's always a way out. We made sure of that."

"You sure?" I asked. "You said you didn't know about the vault."

"True," James replied. "But this one I do know. There's an old maintenance tunnel that leads to the river."

"Like the boathouse," I said, shaking my head. "Always making sure they had escape routes. Well, lead on. Let's get the hell out of here, if we can."

The maintenance tunnel was narrow and steep. Decades of upgrades and repairs were visible to its construction. Modern LED strips mixed with old electrical work told the story of how the families had continuously modernized their escape routes.

"Wait," Sarah whispered, stopping suddenly. She was staring at a series of numbers on the wall. "These match sequences in the diary. Some kind of inventory system."

Behind us, I could hear voices in the vault and I recognized Thomas Mason's voice when he shouted: "They've accessed everything. Initiate Protocol Seven."

"That's bad," James said, his face going pale. "Protocol Seven means…"

The noise of an explosion cut him off.

"That was protocol seven," James said when the noise died down.

The families were collapsing the tunnel network with us still inside it.

"These markings," Sarah said, studying the wall. "I think they're coordinates."

"Geez, Sarah," I snapped. "Leave it. We don't have time for that!"

But Kate was already photographing the markings. "Smart," she said. "Hide the escape route map where they'd never think to look."

"We need to run," James said urgently. "We've got maybe five minutes before they collapse this section."

And we ran.

The shaft ended at a heavy steel door. Fortunately, James's codes still worked. The families either didn't know he'd turned, or they hadn't had time to lock him out of the system.

Beyond the door lay a small dock area, hidden beneath an overhanging rock.

"We maintain these access points carefully," James explained as we emerged. "Weekly shipments still come through here."

"Like the gold during the war," Sarah said.

Kate's police scanner crackled. Fish and Wildlife river patrols were reporting multiple boats converging on our location.

"Let's get out of here," I said. And we did. We scrambled up through the bushes and blackthorn to the road to find we were less than two hundred yards from our vantage point of the previous evening.

"Come on," I shouted, and I ran.

We reached the grassy knoll in record time and hunkered down.

"We need a ride, Kate," I said. "Call it in."

Kate nodded and called dispatch. "Dispatch, this is Sergeant Gazzara," she said. "We... er, need a ride. We're stranded at—" she gave them the location. "Request immediate assistance for four."

"Copy that," the dispatcher responded. "ETA in... twelve minutes."

All was quiet at the Rawlings Mansion when we arrived to drop James off in an unmarked black SUV some thirty minutes later.

"Are you going to be all right?" I asked.

He took a deep breath, locked eyes with me, and then nodded, and I couldn't help but feel sorry for him. He was in a world of trouble.

"You have my number," I said. "If you need me, don't hesitate to call."

Again, he nodded, then turned away and mounted the steps and disappeared into his home. *To what kind of reception?* I wondered as we climbed into my car and drove away back to the PD.

———

BACK IN MY OFFICE, we reorganized what we'd learned about the family structures. The Rawlings family tree sprawled across our evidence board, with Elizabeth at the top, branches extending to her son James Jr., his wife Eleanor, and their son James III.

"Eleanor Rawlings is interesting," Kate noted, studying the board. "She's maintained the perfect society wife image for decades, but almost never appears at family business functions."

"Deliberate distancing or exclusion by the family?" I wondered out loud.

"Hard to say," Kate replied. "According to these society pages, she focuses on charity work, mainly literacy programs and historical preservation."

"Historical preservation," I repeated, something clicking. "Elizabeth's development project involves historical elements. I wonder if Eleanor had any input."

"Might be worth looking into," Kate agreed, "once we've followed more pressing leads."

I made a note to circle back to Eleanor when time permitted. As an in-law who'd observed the family for decades without appearing to be fully a part of said family, she might be able to offer insights others couldn't.

Sarah pulled out the development plans and spread them on the table in front of my desk.

"These aren't standard elevation markers. They're coordinates, dates, vault locations, and... It looks like Elizabeth mapped everything."

"The families think they're erasing everything," Kate said as she photographed the plans. "But not this."

I couldn't help but smile when I realized how Elizabeth had outsmarted them. Even in death, she'd been able to expose the truth about Chattanooga's most powerful families.

It was then that Sarah received a call from a nurse at the Dr. Henry Harvey Psychiatric Facility where her father had been moved to a private room and was being carefully watched. He wanted to see her, and the sympathetic nurse had provided her personal cell number. Sarah called her.

"Nurse Westwood. How can I help you?"

———————

WE ARRIVED some thirty minutes later at eleven-forty-five, and were met at a rear service door by Westwood. "You have ten minutes," she whispered as she let us in. "Security does their rounds on the hour."

Dr. Walker sat propped up in bed, his shoulder bandaged but his mind sharp. "Elizabeth's office," he said, recognizing the diary in Sarah's hands. "You found her safe, then?"

"And we need your help to decode it," I explained, showing him the encrypted entries.

Walker worked quickly despite his injury, identifying key patterns in Emma Rawlings' writings. "It's a classic substitution cipher," he explained. "Elizabeth and I spent weeks breaking it. The diary mentions a pact between the families broken by 'unforgivable betrayal.'"

His expertise proved invaluable as Kate photographed the relevant pages and noted his observations. His academic perspective helped connect historical dots that might have otherwise taken us days to figure out.

"Security will be back soon," Sarah said, checking her watch.

"Here, take this," Walker said as he pressed a flash drive into his daughter's hand. "It contains the research notes I backed up before the shooting. Elizabeth's findings, my analysis, everything."

She nodded, tears in her eyes, leaned over and kissed him on the forehead, and we left, sneaking out the way we'd come, leaving Walker to maintain his cover as a compliant patient while actually serving as our inside source in the families' containment operation.

From the hospital, we went to Kate's apartment, where Sarah

took over Kate's laptop, inserted the flash drive and pulled up her father's research.

"He mentions Clara Mason, Thomas's sister," she said without looking up. "It appears she knew what was going on and kept records as insurance. There are bank transfers, security reports, and photographs showing both families' leaders meeting regularly... Hmm, he doesn't say where. And, from what I can tell, Elizabeth found Clara's records early last month."

Sarah watched as the screens scrolled by, shaking her head. "These accounts are still active," she said. "They're moving millions through the same Swiss banks they used during the war. And then there's this: it says here that Elizabeth contacted the FBI's art theft crime division. Apparently, she'd traced stolen artifacts being moved through their riverfront properties. But when she started linking current crimes to the wartime operation..." She looked up. "It doesn't say what happened. Dad just made a note about finding Elizabeth's historian."

She scrolled through several more screens, then stopped. "Then there's this," she said. "It's about the gold smelting operation. That's what Elizabeth found first. There are records showing that both families were processing Nazi gold during the war, using the Mason textile mill as cover."

"Okay," I said. "That's enough for now. I need a break and so do you. I'm going to take a shower and then get something to eat. I suggest we reconvene at my place in..." I looked at my watch it was just after two o'clock. "At four. You good with that, Kate?"

She nodded. So did Sarah, and I left.

I stopped on the way home and grabbed two extra-large ready to bake pizzas from Murphy's, took my shower, then called the chief. Needless to say, that conversation left me... not exhausted, but certainly a little worse for wear.

8

Friday Afternoon, October 19, 6pm

Kate and Sarah arrived at my condo on the river right on time. I opened the garage for her and she drove in, parked her car next to mine, and I closed the garage door, hoping she hadn't been followed.

I baked the pizzas, opened a nice bottle of Pinot Noir, and the three of us sat down to eat.

Dinner, if you could call it that, lasted less than thirty minutes. I could see that both Sarah and Kate were antsy and wanted to get down to business. So I cleared the table, and we did just that. Kate spread out photographs from the vault.

"These shipping manifests are all recent," she said.

"That's because they never stopped," I said. "I mean, we already know that. And that they just modernized and diversified. When the gold ran out, they turned to stolen art and antiquities smuggling and money laundering."

"What about the historian Dad mentioned?" Sarah asked. "Dr. Robert Thorne. He's an expert in Southern industrial history.

Dad says Elizabeth hired him specifically to trace the families' wartime activities. Don't you think we should talk to him? I mean, like right now?"

I sat back in my chair, blew air out through my teeth, and looked at her. Her eyes were wide with anticipation.

Me? I'd been hoping for a quiet night, an early night, but… I was just about to tell her we'd do it in the morning when I had one of those feelings. Somehow, I knew it was the right thing to do. So we did. I locked everything away in my safe and we headed straight to the University of Tennessee, where Elizabeth's private historian had an office.

It was almost six when we arrived and I wasn't even sure if he'd be there and, in a way, I was right. That's a bit of a twist, I know, but you'll soon understand.

I knew something was wrong the minute we entered the library. I could feel it. It just felt… wrong. It was too quiet, too empty. Campus security should have been at their desk in the lobby, but they weren't. That in itself was an anomaly.

And, sure enough, we found Thorne in his office on the third floor, but he wasn't going to be much help. His body lay sprawled across his desk, surrounded by dozens of old photographs.

"Well, there goes that," Kate said, staring at the body. "Professional hit, d'you think?" she asked, checking the scene.

"Could be," I said, thoughtfully. "Call it in, Kate."

She nodded, took out her phone and called it in while I looked around.

Papers were scattered around everywhere. Someone had searched the place methodically before staging the scene. But then, out of the chaos, one photograph caught my eye: it showed the members of both families together at the Mason mill, dated one week before the fire. *Hmm, interesting,* I thought, frowning. *Why would he have been looking at that particular photo, I wonder?*

"Look at these," Sarah said. "These are ship manifests

disguised as textile orders. And these are German banking records."

"How about this?" Kate called. "I found a laptop. It was hidden on the bookshelf behind the books. You think maybe Thorne backed everything up?"

"Let me see it," Sarah said. "If there are files, I should be able to download them."

"I'm not sure about that," Kate said, reluctantly handing her the laptop. "It's evidence."

"I'm not going to destroy or delete anything," Sarah said, inserting a thumb drive.

"Well, hurry up then," Kate said, frowning. "You've got about ten minutes before CSI gets here."

"I'm going as fast as I can," Sarah muttered as her fingers flew over the keys.

While they worked, I continued to assess the room. As first on the scene, it would be my case, so I wasn't sure why Kate was being so protective of the laptop. Mike Willis would, I was sure, turn it over to us in due course, anyway.

And then, "Quiet!" I snapped. "Listen. Someone's coming and they're in a hurry." I could hear the sound of boots on the stairs.

"They're coming back to destroy the evidence," Sarah said, staring at the screen as the files slowly downloaded.

We'd learn later that the historian's research was damning. Thorne had traced gold shipments from occupied Europe through a complex network to the old mill where it had been smelted and then laundered through subsidiaries in the middle east. Both families had used their legitimate business connections to hide their Nazi collaboration, then maintained those same channels through the years.

The footsteps were in the hallway and getting closer. Through the window, I could see more men covering the exits.

"Got it," Sarah whispered, finishing the download and pulling the thumb drive.

"Okay, now go hide somewhere," I snapped. "We're about to have company."

Sarah scuttled into the bathroom and locked the door.

Kate and I stood with our backs to the wall facing the door, weapons drawn.

The door handle turned. It opened and four men in tactical gear rushed in, weapons at the ready.

"Good afternoon, gentlemen," I said as they halted in front of us. "Sergeant Harry Starke, Chattanooga PD. You just entered a crime scene. Now I suggest you either back off or drop your weapons. Which is it to be?"

They never said a word. At a signal from the leader, they backed slowly out and quietly disappeared, which didn't upset me at all. Two cops with handguns against four obviously well-trained operatives wearing tactical gear and bearing what looked like assault rifles. That would have been a loser for me and Kate. We got lucky; I guess.

By the time Mike Willis and his team arrived some ten minutes later, they were gone, vanished into the night.

Back at Kate's place, we settled in and began to go through the files Sarah had downloaded from Thorne's laptop.

I turned on the Channel 7 evening news. Amanda Cole was reporting Thorne's homicide. Mike Willis and his team were still at the scene, but we knew what they'd find, or rather, wouldn't find. The families were thorough about eliminating evidence.

"Look at this," Sarah said suddenly. "Thorne traced Clara Mason's movements during the mill fire. She wasn't in Chattanooga that night. She was in Switzerland, opening the accounts we're still tracking."

Chapter 8

A knock at the door froze us all. Kate looked at me. I nodded, and she opened the door. James Rawlings III was alone, and he looked nervous.

"What are you doing here, James?" I asked, stepping forward.

"I… I… They're moving too… too… fast now," he stuttered. "They're making mistakes. Margaret Mason is calling an emergency meeting of both families."

"Why tell us?" Kate asked.

"Because Elizabeth was right," he replied. "This has to end. Three generations of lies… it's poisoning everything it touches. Here, this might help."

He handed over a flash drive. "Security footage from the Mason estate," he said nervously. "Proof both families coordinated Elizabeth's murder. And Thorne's." He paused, then continued, "The security agents at the hospital where they're keeping your father work for Mason," James said, looking at Sarah. "The families have people inside multiple agencies, including the police department. Have had for generations. It's how they've stayed ahead of the investigations."

I locked eyes with him. I didn't know why, but somehow I didn't trust him. Was it his nervous disposition, or was it something else? I didn't know, so I said, "Thank you, James, but you need to go home now. This is not the place you need to be. Come by my office tomorrow morning and we'll talk."

He nodded and, reluctantly, I thought and left.

We spent the next hour working through both James' and Thorne's files. The footage James had supplied showed the family leaders meeting the night before Elizabeth died, planning her elimination. And that was as far as we got, because it was then that headlights swept the apartment windows.

"They must have followed him," I snapped. "The son of a bitch led them right to us."

"You don't know that," Kate said. "My address is not a secret."

"Whatever," I snapped. "We need to get out of here, now."

"Through the garage," Kate said. "We're going to have to bust out of here."

Kate hit the garage door button as she ran, and we reversed both cars out onto the street together, sirens blaring, lights flashing, one going one way, the other going the other, taking the would-be intruders completely by surprise.

I grabbed my radio and called for emergency backup to Kate's apartment and we made our separate ways to my condo.

By the time we arrived, I was totally washed out. I'd had just about enough for one day, and I said so, but Sarah was insistent we spend the rest of the evening analyzing Thorne's research. "The historian found a pattern," Sarah explained, tiredly. "Every time someone got close to exposing them, the families staged a public battle to distract attention."

"Like they're doing now," I muttered. "But we already knew that, didn't we? Tomorrow's news will be full of stories about both families accusing each other of God only knows what. Geez, this is turning out to be one convoluted messed up…" I trailed off and heaved a sigh.

"Yes, but Elizabeth had outsmarted them," Sarah, continued, despite my obvious irritation. "Between Thorne's research, Walker's evidence, and the development plans, she left a trail they couldn't erase. Don't you get it?"

I got it. The truth about Chattanooga's most powerful families was finally beginning to emerge.

The question was, though, how many more would have to die before we could stop them?

THE NORTH SHORE CONSPIRACY
Saturday morning, October 20

MOST WEEKENDS, when I'm not busy with a case, I work Saturday morning and play golf on Sunday with my father and his friends. That weekend, however, there would be no time off. The chief was on my ass almost constantly and I had to work the two cases —Elizabeth's and Robert Thorne's murders—to a satisfactory conclusion, whatever the hell that meant. So, Kate and I rose early that Saturday morning and went into the office, leaving Sarah at my condo to do what she did best, research.

Me? I spent the morning reviewing Elizabeth Rawlings' development, the plans spread across my desk in what would one day become Kate's office, the sunlight shining through the window illuminating what had initially looked to me like standard architectural drawings but now revealed something far more intricate and… encoded.

"These elevation markers make no sense," I muttered as Kate walked in with coffee.

"Two hours of sleep doesn't help your analytical skills," she replied, setting a steaming cup beside me. Dark circles under her eyes told me she had fared little better than I had. After the confrontation at her apartment, we'd both been running on fumes.

"Don't exaggerate," I said, grinning at her. "It wasn't my fault you—"

"Stop!" she snapped. "We don't discuss our private life at work, remember?"

"Yes, I remember. Come look at this," I said, pointing to a series of numerical notations in the margins. "These aren't standard survey points. The measurements are too precise, and they don't match the topography."

Kate leaned over my shoulder, her perfume a momentary distraction. "They almost look like geographic coordinates," she said, frowning.

I took another breath of her perfume, a sip of my third cup of coffee that morning, and nodded, the caffeine finally kick-starting my brain. "She wasn't just planning construction, was she?" I mused. "She was mapping something."

"The old tunnel system, I think," Kate said, tracing a pattern across the blueprint. "She's marked specific access points that correspond with properties the families have fought over."

"Yeah," I replied, "but most of them have been destroyed."

I thought for a moment, then said, "You know, we need to get Sarah out of my condo. If they find her there, she could be in serious trouble."

"How about a hotel?" Kate asked.

I nodded. "That sounds like a plan. See to it, will you, please?"

She nodded, and I called Sarah Walker and told her a car was on the way to pick her up and to bring her things with her and make sure my place was securely locked up before she left.

She arrived forty minutes later with her laptop, the diary, and her father's research.

"The historian found something specific," she said without preamble. "They're moving an art shipment next week. That's why they're moving so fast. And Elizabeth's development project was specifically designed to expose the foundations of the old Mason mill," she continued as she set her laptop on a clear spot on the round table in front of the desk.

"Geez, Sarah," Kate said. "Slow down. You'll give yourself a heart attack, the rate you're going. By the way, I've booked you into the Marriot until this thing is sorted out."

Sarah smiled at her self-consciously. "Thanks. Sorry, I do tend to get a little carried away, don't I? So, what are we doing?"

"We're comparing this to this," I said as I overlayed the historical maps with the blueprints Mike Willis had retrieved from the Robert Thorne crime scene. He'd dropped them off just after we arrived that morning.

Sarah leaned over my desk and, with her finger, traced the main excavation area. "This section aligns perfectly with where the sub-levels would have been."

"Sub-levels not on the official records," I noted, remembering the blueprints we'd seen at Dr. Walker's office.

Sarah nodded. "According to my father's research, something was hidden there during the war. Something the families never moved."

My desk phone rang. It was the front desk announcing James Rawlings III had arrived. I'd been surprised when I first realized that the man had seemed to have turned, and I wasn't happy the way the security team had arrived at Kate's apartment less than an hour after he left, but I was prepared to give him a shot at redemption, if that's what he was after.

"Send him up," I said.

James looked like hell. The polished appearance had given way to someone who'd spent the night looking over his shoulder.

"I want protection," were the first words out of his mouth as he sat down at the table.

"That depends on you," I replied. "And what you bring to the table."

"My grandmother had evidence of treason," he said after I let the silence stretch uncomfortably long. "She had documents showing Mason collaboration with German industrial firms before and after Pearl Harbor."

"Just the Masons?" Kate asked, pointedly, from her position against the wall.

James's hesitation told me everything. "Both families," he finally admitted, staring at his hands. "The feud was always just for show."

"So Elizabeth was going to expose you?" I said.

"She designed the development project specifically to uncover the mill foundations. There are sealed vaults still down there that connect directly to the families' operations. They built reinforced storage chambers when they constructed the mill."

I stared at him for a moment. I still didn't trust him, but what he said could easily be confirmed. So, giving him the benefit of the doubt, I immediately issued orders to secure the development site, but when we arrived there less than thirty minutes later, we found construction had mysteriously resumed overnight.

"What the hell?" I said, getting out of my car.

The two uniformed officers I'd stationed at the site approached, looking uncomfortable.

"Orders came down from upstairs, Sarge," Officer Davis explained. "Chief Johnston authorized resumption of work after receiving calls from…" he hesitated, then said, "concerned parties with significant influence."

While James and Sarah remained in the car out of sight, from our position on the perimeter, Kate and I watched security teams from both families supervising workers around a specific section of the old mill foundation.

"They're removing something," Kate said, focusing her binoculars.

My construction contact, Jim Stanfield, approached, keeping his head down. "We found a sealed vault in the foundation yesterday," he muttered. "There's an old steel door with some kind of locking mechanism. It's pretty rusted, but before we could document it properly, these security people showed up with paperwork and took over."

"What kind of paperwork?" I asked, holding out my hand.

"Something about historical preservation," he replied as he handed it to me. "They said the site contains artifacts of historical significance that fall under federal protection laws."

I glanced at it, then handed the two sheets of paper to Kate.

"It looks legitimate to me, Harry," she said. "They're smart. They're using the National Historic Preservation Act to control access."

"How damn convenient," I replied.

We watched as workers carefully excavated around what appeared to be a small vault door built into the foundation. The surrounding concrete was being removed with jack hammers.

"They're treating it like an archaeological dig," Kate said.

"Making it look official," I agreed.

A black SUV arrived, and James Rawlings Jr, our James' father, emerged with Thomas Mason. The patriarchs were together again, their decades-old feud apparently forgotten.

"Look at them," I said to Kate. "Three generations of public hatred evaporating the minute their precious secrets are threatened."

A city-issue Crown Victoria screeched to a halt nearby, and Lieutenant Jack "Bull" Marshall lumbered out.

Jack was, as his nickname indicated, a bull of a man: six-two, hefty at two-hundred-forty pounds, brown hair, heavy brows and jowls, a nose like a white strawberry, and beady black eyes. Put it all together and you had a nasty piece of work consumed by his own self-importance. Needless to say, he and I didn't get along.

"You're off this site, Starke," he barked, walking up to us with the swagger of a man enjoying himself too much. "Chief's direct order. This is now a heritage preservation matter. Not your jurisdiction."

"A murder investigation trumps preservation concerns," I snapped, standing my ground, but knowing I was on a loser to nothing.

"Not according to the federal statutes they're citing." His smile didn't reach his eyes. "And the chief wants you and Gazzara back at the station now."

I felt Kate's hand on my arm, a silent warning not to push it. She was right, of course. This wasn't the hill I wanted to die on.

We retreated to my car, watching Marshall strut back toward the patriarchs like an eager lapdog.

"Heritage preservation, my ass," Kate said.

"And a lovely ass it is too," I said as I opened my door.

"You don't seem too bothered," she said as she slid into the passenger seat.

"I never worry about things I can't change; you know that," I said as I started the engine. "And anyway, they've been using preservation laws for years to maintain control of key properties. Now they're using those same laws to sanitize evidence."

"So what now?" Kate asked, her frustration matching my own. "He said the chief wants us back at the office."

"Did he, now?" I said and grinned at her as I pulled away from the site, my mind already working the angles. "I don't know, Kate," I replied, letting my frustration show. "Elizabeth Rawlings knew what they were up to. Which is why she encoded the evidence. Whatever's in that vault, we'll never know. For all intents and purposes, we should probably regard it as nothing more than bait."

"Bait?" she asked. "What are you talking about?"

"To force them to react, to mobilize their resources, to force them to expose themselves." I glanced at her. "And they already did, didn't they? We need to look at the rest of her development plans. I mean, she was mapping more than just the mill site, wasn't she? In the meantime, as you say, I have a date with the chief. You want in?" I glanced at her and grinned, already knowing the answer.

"Not hardly," she replied, settling comfortably into her seat.

"Thought not," I said. "You ready?"

"Always," she replied and closed her eyes.

THE MISTAKE
Saturday morning, October 20

THE MIDDAY SUN glinted off the Tennessee River as we drove along Riverfront Parkway back toward the PD. Beneath the city proper, portions of the old city remained somewhat intact despite the families' attempts to collapse key sections. Elizabeth Rawlings had died trying to expose it all. And despite their money, their connections, and their three generations of deception, I wasn't about to let her death go unanswered or unpunished.

"The families think they control the narrative," I said, as I turned in toward the lot at the rear of the building. "But Elizabeth was smarter than all of them. She knew exactly how they'd respond."

"And she left us a map, bless her," Kate finished, without opening her eyes.

"Hey," I said, nudging her with my elbow. "Wake up. We're here."

"I'm not asleep," she protested. "I was just resting my eyes."

"Yeah, right," I said, as I opened the car door.

I asked Kate to take James and Sarah to my office, and, as we were already in the corridor outside the chief's suite of offices, I told Kate to go on up and I'd join them when I got through with the chief, and then I walked confidently into the lion's den.

"He's expecting you," Cindy, his secretary, said. "Go on in."

And I did.

"What the hell is going on, Starke?" he snapped, the grand mustache literally bristling.

Without being asked, I flopped tiredly down in the chair in front of his desk and did my best to bring him up to speed, with a little theory thrown in for good measure.

By the time I'd finished, he seemed to have calmed down some.

"I don't like it, Harry," he began. "These people, and the mayor, are all over me. The Masons and the Rawlings both want me to fire you—"

"And there you have it, Chief," I replied, interrupting him; something I rarely ever did. "I'm investigating Elizabeth Rawlings' murder. Why would they want me fired? Unless I'm getting too close. Look, they're all complicit in a major, seven-decades-old criminal enterprise that Elizabeth was planning to expose that evening. It's classic. You of all people know that. They're cleaning up, Chief. They're hiding or destroying the evidence. I'm making waves, Chief."

"Then you better be careful you don't drown yourself in the process. Now get out of here. Get this thing solved, and quickly, before we all get fired."

"You got it, Chief," I said, then added, "One last thing—"

"What?" he snapped.

"Jack Marshall. I want him off my back."

He nodded. "I'll see to it."

And with that, I walked jauntily out of his office, smiled

sweetly at Cindy, then took the elevator up to the incident room and my office.

"Don't," I said as I stepped into my office. Sarah immediately opened her mouth to speak. "I appreciate your enthusiasm, but I need a moment to think."

I went to my desk, sat down, and stared at the twin white-boards bearing the photos of Elizabeth Rawlings, Robert Thorne, the two patriarchs, James III, Margaret Mason, the old family photograph, and I shook my head.

"We're in trouble, people," I said. "The chief is about to blow his lid, and we're no closer to solving this mess than we were last Monday. We know who's responsible for the two deaths—at least we think we do—but we can't prove it. All we have is your father's research, Dr. Thorne's research, and Emma Rawlings' diary. All that provides us with is theory, and theory is not acceptable in a court of law. We need hard evidence." I paused and looked first at Kate, then at Sarah.

They both remained silent for a moment, then Kate frowned and said, "What about the bogus security outfits…?"

"Bogus?" I asked impatiently. "They're legitimate, indepen-dent private security companies, part of the families' conglomerates."

"But the research—" Sarah said.

"That's all it is," I snapped, cutting her off. "And circumstantial at best.

"Look," I continued, "the focus has to be on who killed Eliza-beth Rawlings and why. We know the answers to both questions. She was killed by someone either employed by, or part of, one or both of the families. Now we need proof."

I leaned back in my chair, locked my hands together behind my neck, and stared up at the ceiling.

"I agree," Kate said, "but we just have to keep at it. You know how these things go, Harry. We keep pushing until something breaks."

I leaned forward, nodded, looked at Sarah, and said, "You were about to say something when I came in. What was it?"

"I was going to say you were right," she replied. "There's more to these blueprints than just construction plans."

I got up, locked the door and pulled the blinds. This wasn't information I wanted wandering through the department, especially with Marshall's sudden interest.

"Show me," I said, setting my coffee down.

Sarah pointed to specific notation patterns. "These aren't just elevation markers. They're coordinates disguised as construction data. And look here," she pointed to a series of numbers along the river portion of the development. "These match dates in my father's research about shipment schedules."

"She embedded a timeline," Kate said, leaning closer.

"And a map," Sarah added. "Elizabeth knew exactly where the evidence was hidden. The vault at the mill site is just one location."

"Stop," I said. "All this research, maps, blueprints, I'm up to here with it. I've had enough of it. How does any of this help us find Elizabeth's killer?"

"It helps establish a pattern..." Kate began then trailed off when she saw the look I was giving her.

"And there are six more," Sarah continued, unabashed, marking points on a city map with a red pen. "All on property controlled by both families through shell companies. All connected to what's left of the tunnel system."

My phone rang. It was the chief. "What the hell?" I muttered. "I only just spoke to him."

I stepped outside to take it.

"Chief?" I said.

"I forgot to tell you, you're to stay away from the mill site and the construction site on Cameron Hill. Understood?"

"Yes, but—"

"I mean it, Harry," he snapped, cutting me off. "Stay away from those two sites." And he hung up.

I took a deep breath, shook my head, and went back into my office.

"Harry," Kate said. "I just got a call from Jack Marshall. Johnston's put him in charge of liaison with the federal preservation team. He's cutting us out of the mill site investigation."

"Of course he is," I muttered.

I studied the map Sarah had prepared. The locations formed a pattern around the city, each one connected to a historic property the families had publicly feuded over while secretly keeping joint control. I closed my eyes, shook my head, and heaved a sigh.

"What's our next move?" Kate asked.

I tapped one of the locations on the map, an old riverfront warehouse off West 19th Street that had passed back and forth between the families for decades, the site of one of their most public legal battles.

"We follow Elizabeth's lead," I said. "Tonight, after Marshall's gone home to his whiskey and regrets."

"And what about protection for me?" James Rawlings III asked from the corner chair where he'd been silently observing.

I'd almost forgotten he was there. "Kate will get you a hotel room. You're to make no contact with anyone, not even family. Understand?"

"They're all family," he said with unexpected bitterness. "That's the problem. The Masons, the Rawlings... we're more connected than anyone knows."

"That didn't stop them from killing your grandmother," I reminded him.

He narrowed his eyes, and again I wondered... "She broke the rules," he said, bitterly. "She threatened the arrangement that kept both our families wealthy and protected for three generations."

"And you?" Kate asked. "You're also breaking the rules. Why now?"

James stared at his hands for a long moment, then said, "I told you. Because she was right. It's gone on long enough." He shook his head. "It's got to stop."

"Tell me about the security teams," I said.

"Rawlings and Mason security companies," he said. "They're legitimate companies. They employ ex-military personnel, ex-special forces, most of them."

I stared at him. I sure as hell didn't trust his sudden conversion, but we needed his knowledge. So while Kate made a reservation at the Marriott, I arranged for a protective detail to take him there, making sure only officers I knew personally were selected for the detail.

As evening fell, Kate, Sarah and I prepared to visit the riverfront warehouse. The families had their resources, but we had something they didn't. We had Elizabeth Rawlings' message, hidden in plain sight within her development plans.

I thought of Elizabeth Rawlings dying in my arms, and I was pissed. A grand old lady whose last act was to hand me the key to unraveling decades of deception.

"Because she was smarter than all of them," I muttered to myself. "And they've finally made a mistake."

"What are you talking about, Harry?" Kate asked. "What mistake?"

"Elizabeth Rawlings," I replied. "They killed the one person who could have kept their secrets hidden forever." I started the car. "Now it's just a matter of time before I put 'em where they belong, behind bars."

11

Saturday Evening, October 20

The warehouse loomed against the night sky, a hulking shadow where the Tennessee River curved toward the city. Kate cut the headlights as we approached and parked behind an abandoned shipping container three hundred yards out from our target. The moon was nearly full, casting enough light for us to see, but not enough to make us visible from that distance.

"There are security cameras on all four corners," she said, studying the building through night-vision binoculars. "And motion sensors along the fence line. I see two guards at the main entrance, and two more patrolling the perimeter."

"For a supposedly abandoned property, they're taking security pretty damn seriously," I remarked, checking my weapon before securing it in my shoulder holster.

According to the property records, this warehouse had passed back and forth between the Masons and Rawlings a dozen times since 1950, each transfer marked by a public legal battle that made headlines. The families, so it seemed, had created the perfect smokescreen by fighting over a building they actually shared.

"There's supposed to be a basement," Sarah whispered.

"Accessible from the old tunnel system?" Kate asked.

Sarah nodded. "What's left of it. This section wasn't destroyed in the collapses we witnessed."

The original tunnel network, connected to the underground city, had been extensive, connecting various properties throughout downtown Chattanooga. Urban renewal had destroyed most of it, and the families had collapsed more sections in recent days, but the essential infrastructure remained intact.

Kate's police scanner crackled softly; routine patrol chatter, nothing concerning our location. I'd been careful not to let anyone know my plan for the night. The fewer people who knew what we were doing, the better. Especially so after what we'd seen at the development site. I couldn't be sure who might be watching.

We'd been watching for almost an hour when Kate said, "It looks like the security rotation is every thirty minutes. Two-man teams. "

I checked my watch. "Okay," I said. "We move after the next rotation. Ten minutes from now."

We used the time to review what we knew. Elizabeth had sent us there because there was something in that warehouse that connected the families' historical crimes to their current operations. The coordinates disguised as elevation markers had been specific. They pointed to the southwest corner of the basement level.

"They've owned this property continuously since 1950," Sarah said, consulting her notes on her laptop. "It's the only location that's never actually changed hands despite the public court battles."

"The perfect cover," Kate said. "Everyone's been so focused on the legal infighting, they've never questioned why both families want it so badly."

"What better place to hide shared assets than in plain sight?" I said. "A property everyone thinks they're fighting over."

I studied Sarah's face in the dim light. The academic researcher had transformed over the past few days into someone harder, someone more determined. Her father's shooting and Thorne's murder had changed her. I recognized the look. I'd seen it before in enough victims who'd become crusaders and, inwardly, I shook my head, hoping her newfound resolve wouldn't get her killed.

"It's time," Kate said, closing her binoculars as the security team completed its rotation.

We moved quickly across the open ground, staying in the shadow of the warehouse, approaching the chain-link fence from its darkest corner. Years of working together made Kate and me an efficient team; she handled the security cameras while I created an entry point in the fence. Sarah followed close behind, clutching the laptop containing Elizabeth's plans.

Inside the perimeter, we hugged the warehouse wall, avoiding the motion sensors Kate had mapped during our observations. The service door on the south side was padlocked, but it took Kate only a few minutes to pick it; something she'd learned years ago from an expert, an expert now serving five years for his indiscretions.

"You never cease to amaze me," I muttered as we slipped inside.

"You're welcome," she murmered.

The interior smelled of dust and old metal. The place seemed to have been abandoned long ago. Our flashlight beams revealed a vast, empty storage area, or what was obviously meant to appear as such. High ceilings disappeared into the darkness overhead. The concrete floor was scuffed from decades of use, and the metal shelving units stood mostly empty along the walls.

"This way," Sarah whispered, and we followed her to a freight elevator hidden behind multiple stacks of age-old wooden pallets.

"I guess this would have provided access for moving heavy cargo," Kate said as she examined the mechanism. "It's still operational," she muttered. "Recently serviced, too, by the look of the hydraulics."

I checked the control panel. "Hah!" I whispered. "No key required. They must be confident about their security."

The elevator groaned as we descended to the basement level. The sensation of dropping below the city level reminded me of the tunnel system we'd navigated days earlier. *Geez, yet another layer of Chattanooga hidden beneath its surface.*

When the doors opened, we found ourselves in a different world. The basement was clean, but damp. *Due to its close proximity to the river,* I thought as I looked around at the new and expensive-looking crates stacked against the wall.

"They're still using it," Kate whispered.

"Looks that way," I said. "What's in the crates, I wonder."

"Over there," Sarah said as she almost ran toward the southwest corner, where a steel-reinforced door stood half-concealed behind a row of filing cabinets. "This is it," she said

The door was old but strong and the lock required an actual key.

"Old tech," I said, looking at Kate.

She smiled and once again produced her set of picks.

But this time it wasn't so easy. It took her nearly ten minutes of careful, painstaking work before we heard the satisfying click of the tumblers falling into place. She grabbed the handle and pulled, and the heavy door swung open to reveal a vault-like room lined with steel boxes. They looked like safe deposit boxes, but obviously weren't bank grade.

"Geez," Sarah breathed.

"Jackpot," Kate said triumphantly.

"Wow!" was all I could come up with.

The boxes were numbered chronologically, starting with 1947. Each decade had its own section, continuing all the way to the present year, 2006. The organization was meticulous; obviously the work of people who expected their secrets to remain hidden.

"This must be one of their archives," I said. "We may not have much time, so let's get started."

We started with the earliest boxes, which required no keys, their locks having long since been disabled, probably for easier access to the contents.

Inside the first few boxes we found leather-bound ledgers documenting gold transfers through Swiss accounts, each entry meticulously recording each family's shares.

"The original blood money," Kate said, photographing the pages. "German gold moving through shell companies, emerging as legitimate business investments."

The earliest records were surprisingly candid, naming German industrialists directly and detailing transactions that occurred before America entered the war. There was no attempt to disguise the nature of these dealings. It was obvious the families had been confident that what they were doing during those early days before the war was legal, and that no one would ever see these records.

"Look at these signatures," Sarah said, pointing to documents from 1941. "Both family patriarchs signing the same agreements with German representatives."

"We need to take those with us," I said. "We've been wanting evidence; this is it."

More recent boxes revealed the evolution of their operation from gold to art and antiquities smuggling, money laundering and financial fraud. The recording methods had modernized through the years, but the operations remained essentially unchanged.

One ledger from 1965 detailed the transformation of their business model: "The operations were diversified following the intense scrutiny of their Swiss accounts," I said. "The art acquisition program was expanded to include archaeological artifacts from Mediterranean sources," I said and looked up at Kate.

"Yeah, I know," she replied, her camera clicking, her voice a mixture of disgust and admiration. "They documented everything. I'm sure they must be proud of it."

"Yeah, right!" I muttered as I pulled another box.

The most recent boxes required keys, but they quickly fell to Kate's picks. Many of them contained digital storage: old external hard drives, Compact Flash cards, SD drives, flash drives, even floppy disks.

"Look at this," Kate said, "These are records from 2004, just two years ago. "Transfers to the same Swiss accounts they were using in 1947."

"Well, we already know they never closed them," I said, stating the obvious.

The financial web was intricate but consistent: assets were moved through shell companies to finally emerge as legitimate investments, then the generated profits were split between both families according to a formula established in 1947.

My phone vibrated - a text from our surveillance team watching James Rawlings at the hotel and the family compounds. All was clear at the hotel, but they reported unusual activity at both family compounds. The security teams were mobilizing.

"They know we're onto something," I said. "We need to move fast."

Kate had found a hidden compartment behind one of the filing cabinets. Inside was a metal lockbox containing what appeared to be original banking documents from the 1940s.

"And these are transfer certificates," Sarah said, examining the yellowed pages. "Proof of how the Nazi gold entered the American banking system through both families' legitimate businesses."

The certificates bore the stamps of now-defunct banks, official seals, and signatures from long-dead bankers who had facilitated the transfers. Several documents showed direct connections to Swiss accounts still active in the families' current operations.

"And this is what connects it all to the present," Kate added, sorting through the more modern banking records. "The flow of assets never stopped."

A file from the 1970s detailed how the families had weathered increased international scrutiny following the collapse of several Swiss banking secrecy laws. They'd created new corporate entities, established new trusts in emerging tax havens, and diversified into art and antiquities; commodities that could be moved without the same financial oversight as currency.

"I think Elizabeth must have found this place," I said, thinking out loud. "And that's probably why they killed her."

"My father tracked inquiries Elizabeth made to these Swiss banks," Sarah said. "He thinks she was building a case for federal prosecutors."

"Smart woman," Kate remarked. "Going after the money, not just the history."

"Follow the money," I agreed. "The one trail that never lies. We need to get the hell out of here while we still can. Grab what you can and that box and let's go."

"Wait," Kate said, continuing to photograph the documents. "We may not get a chance like this again."

We photographed everything we could systematically, making sure to document the continuity between historical records and current operations.

A soft alarm chimed from Kate's phone. "Security is changing rotation early. Something's spooked them," she said.

"It's time to go," I said. "Wrap this up, now!"

We retraced our steps, closing the vault door behind us, and we ran to the elevator. I hit the button, and the door closed. As it opened on the main floor, we could see headlights flashing across the warehouse windows. We were too late.

"It looks like we've got company," Kate whispered. "What now, Harry?"

Through a dust-covered window, I could see three black SUVs pulling up outside. "Family security," I said. "There must be a back exit." I looked around. "That way," I said. "Come on," and we ran toward what I assumed must be the loading docks.

"There," I snapped, and ran to the door only to find it locked. "Damn!" I muttered as I looked around. "We're trapped!"

Kate looked at me, her hand on her weapon. Sarah looked at me. Even in the shadows I could see how pale her face was; the poor kid was scared.

"Plan B," I muttered, grabbing them both by the arms and pulling them toward a storage area filled with empty shipping crates.

We hunkered down behind a stack of pallets as the main doors opened and the beams of flashlights swept the vast open space. Voices echoed throughout the warehouse as they began what appeared to be a systematic sweep.

"They must know we're here," Kate whispered as she pulled her weapon and checked the load.

I nodded grimly and said, "But they don't know what we found."

Sarah clutched her laptop. She was also wearing a backpack containing the box and the digital evidence: the memory cards containing hundreds of photographs and the damning financial records.

Through gaps between the pallets, I could see six men moving through the warehouse. Their gear was unmarked, but the way they conducted themselves smacked of military training. They were obviously members of the families' private security agencies.

Footsteps approached our position. I signaled Kate to circle left while I moved right, creating distance between us and Sarah, hoping to draw attention away from the evidence.

I made my move first, emerging from cover with my badge in my hand clearly visible. "Sergeant Starke, Chattanooga PD, Homicide! What's the meaning of…" I waved my hand, "this?"

The security team leader, a hefty former military type with cold eyes, barely reacted. "This is private property, Sergeant Starke. You're trespassing."

"I'm investigating a homicide," I countered, keeping his attention on me while Kate moved into position. "Elizabeth Rawlings. Perhaps you've heard of her?"

"We have authorization to secure this building," he replied mechanically. "All unauthorized visitors are to be escorted off the premises."

"Show me that authorization and your ID," I demanded, forcing him to reach for his documentation.

That moment of distraction was all Kate needed. She emerged from the shadows, weapon in her right hand, flanking the security team. "Sergeant Gazzara," she snapped, her badge raised in her left hand. "Everyone stay calm. We don't want any nasty, inexplicable incidents, now do we? Backup is on the way"

It was a calculated risk. She was reminding them that an assault on police officers would bring scrutiny no one wanted, and that our people knew where we were.

The security leader reassessed the situation, then made a decision.

"You have five minutes to leave the premises," he snapped. "After that, our orders are absolute."

We took the offer, moving calmly toward the exit, retrieving

Sarah from her hiding place along the way. Incredibly, no one tried to search us. No one demanded to see what we'd found. They obviously wanted us gone more than they wanted a confrontation.

Once outside, we walked quickly to our car.

Me? I could feel their eyes tracking our every move. Only when we were five miles away did I finally allow myself to relax.

"That was too easy," Kate said, voicing my own concern.

"They were following protocol," Sarah said. "I'd say they're instructed to avoid direct confrontation whenever possible."

"Smart thinking," I admitted. "It would be hard to claim harassment when they're being technically cooperative."

"Why risk a scene when they can clean up after we leave?" Kate added.

"Except we've already got what we came for," I said, glancing in the mirror at Sarah, who was still wearing her backpack.

Still, the ease of our escape troubled me. These were people who had maintained a complex criminal enterprise for decades. They didn't make mistakes. Which meant either we weren't as big a threat as we thought we were, or they were confident they could contain whatever it was we'd discovered.

Back at my riverside condo, we spread out the evidence on my dining table. The financial records we found in the box told a damning story: millions of dollars flowing through numbered accounts and then laundered through multiple offshore shell companies had been transformed over the years into respectable family wealth.

As we began to analyze the financial records, I noticed a pattern in the trust documentation.

"Look at these charitable donations," I said, pointing to a series of transfers. "All to historical preservation projects, all approved with the same signature: E.R."

Kate leaned closer. "Elizabeth Rawlings... No, wait. Eleanor Rawlings, d'you think?"

"Could be," I replied. "If so, she's been directing the family trust money to preservation projects for twenty years."

"Including projects that would have raised questions about family properties," Kate noted. "That's either a remarkable coincidence or..."

"Or she knows more than she's letting on," I finished. "Eleanor Rawlings just moved up our interview list."

"D'you think maybe she could have been working with Elizabeth?"

I considered the possibility. "It's possible, I suppose, but at this point, we shouldn't make assumptions..." I said. I thought for a moment, squinted, pursed my lips, slowly shaking my head, then continued, "Eh... but the timing of some of these donations aligns suspiciously with Elizabeth's research timeline."

It was time to have a conversation with the woman who'd navigated the Rawlings families' financial waters for more than thirty years.

"What's most impressive is the consistency of it all," Kate said, as she reviewed the documents. "Same structure, same division of profits, same operational security for over seventy years."

"Family business," I said. "Passed down from one generation to the next."

"These account numbers match transfers my father traced to art acquisitions in the 1980s," Sarah mused. "Pieces that disappeared from European collections during the war suddenly reappearing in private collections decades later."

"What you're saying is that they've been laundering looted art, then?" Kate said.

"And using the profits to fund legitimate business ventures," I added. "Creating a cycle of criminality that's almost impossible to detect, if you don't know where to look."

The scope of the organization was staggering. Not just the initial Nazi collaboration, but the decades of systematic criminal activity disguised as legitimate business. This was a crime family that rivaled any New York had to offer.

"Blood money," I said, examining a transfer certificate bearing both family crests. "Built into the foundation of everything both families own."

My phone rang. It was James Rawlings III, and he sounded agitated.

12

LOOT
Saturday Evening, October 20

"HARRY. They know you've been to the warehouse," he said. "They're pissed off and they're worried. They're speeding things up. They're closing down and clearing the evidence from all of the locations my grandmother identified."

"How do you know?" I asked, suspicious.

"I still have contacts inside," he replied. "Listen, they're moving a shipment of art tomorrow night. They're clearing everything out before the feds can get search warrants. My source told me they think Grandmother Elizabeth set up some sort of dead man's switch, and the information was automatically released to the feds after her death. You have to give it to the old girl; she knew they'd kill her if they had to, so she made sure the evidence would survive."

The sophistication of Elizabeth's planning impressed me.

"Where's the shipment coming from?" I asked.

"There's a vault beneath the downtown Mason Building. It's

where they store the most valuable pieces. They know they're in trouble, Harry, and that the feds are closing in, so they're moving everything out of the country. They already have buyers for most of it."

"All right, James," I said. "Stay where you are until you hear from me."

After I hung up, I shared the information with Kate and Sarah.

"Wow," Kate said when I'd finished. "Elizabeth was one smart lady."

"That she was," I replied.

"The question is, what are we going to do about it?" Kate asked.

"Give me a minute," I replied. "I need to think."

"Maybe she was trying to build a RICO case," Sarah said, her eyes widening. "You know, the Racketeer Influenced and Corrupt Organizations Act."

"Could be," I replied.

"I'm thinking wire fraud, as well as dealing in Nazi loot," Kate said, thoughtfully. "Could they be charged with war crimes by The International War Crimes Commission, I wonder?"

I stared at her and slowly shook my head. "That would be a bit of a stretch, don't you think?"

"Not really," she replied. "From what I know, the commission was established after the war to prosecute war crimes committed by Nazi Germany and… other… Axis…" She trailed off, staring at me. "What?" she asked. "What are you smiling at?"

I shook my head. "As I've said many a time, you never cease to amaze me, Kate."

"Yeah, well," she muttered, blushing, then changed the subject. "How old was she?" Kate asked.

I grinned across the table at her. "Seventy-four."

She just shook her head and said, "I hope I'm that good when I'm that age… if I reach that age."

"What you said," Sarah said, smiling for the first time since I'd met her. "I like the war crimes idea, though."

"We need to find out what the FBI's up to," I said, and I called the local field office. After a lot of finagling, I managed to get through to Carl Boem, the SAIC who, after even more finagling and a call to the PD, confirmed his office had already secured search warrants for several properties based on Elizabeth's evidence, and that the investigation had been proceeding quietly until Elizabeth's murder had accelerated the timeline.

I put him on speaker.

"We, along with FBI Art Crimes, have been building a case against the two families for months," Boem said. "Elizabeth Rawlings was our primary CA."

"So what you're telling me," I said. "is that someone found out what she was up to and silenced her?"

"Looks that way," Boem replied. "As you're the lead detective in her homicide investigation, I should probably have read you in," he continued, "but… well. You know how that goes, right?"

"Oh yeah," I replied, dryly. "I know only too well. When are you intending to serve the warrants?" I asked.

"We still have a few loose ends to tie up," he replied. "but sometime tomorrow would be my best guess. You want to come along?"

"Let me think about it," I said."

"Let me know," he replied. "Have a good evening, Detective."

"Why didn't you tell him about the shipment?" Sarah asked.

"Why didn't he tell me about his investigation?" I retorted.

Kate smiled.

"The FBI and the police," she said, "we don't get along, Sarah."

"Yes, I heard about that, but I thought it was just a load of BS," Sarah said. "I mean, why wouldn't law enforcement agencies cooperate? It makes no sense that they don't."

"Why indeed," Kate muttered, leaning back in her chair, arms folded, watching her.

"Anyway," Sarah continued, "going through my father's research, I found something else; a detailed inventory of what's in the Mason building vault. I think it must be something Elizabeth gave him. It's an itemized list of artifacts, including several pieces long thought lost after World War II. Paintings from Jewish collections seized by the Nazis," she said, scrolling through the list. "And ancient artifacts looted from museums during the occupation."

I poured myself a glass of scotch and went out onto the patio. I was stumped. My mind was in a whirl. I needed a break to clear my head.

I rarely get emotional about my cases but, as I sat alone, glass in hand, watching the reflections on the surface of the water, I couldn't help but feel sorry for Elizabeth, and what had happened to her, and I wished I could have known her. It was a moment, but it didn't last long and ten minutes later, I was back at the table, working through the evidence, slowly piecing together the story of the two families whose public hatred of one another had masked decades of criminal collaboration. But I still couldn't get it out of my head how Elizabeth Rawlings had died in my arms trying to expose the truth. It was at that moment I decided what to do.

"Tomorrow night's shipment," I said, "That's our opportunity."

"To do what?" Kate asked.

"To catch them in the act," I said. "My guess is they'll move it out through the underground… what's left of it," I muttered. "If so, according to these blueprints, the only place they can go is here." I tapped the location of the boathouse.

"The downtown Mason Building is right above the underground," I continued, "and, according to James, they're already making preparations to move the stuff. I only hope he's not lying to us. But be that as it may, we have to assume that he's on the up and up." I looked at Kate, then continued, "We know they use the river for transport, so, if we coordinate with Agent Boem we can catch them with the stolen artwork."

Sarah looked uncertain. "I think maybe you're assuming too much," she said. "These are powerful people, and they're not stupid."

"Which is why we need irrefutable evidence," I replied. "We need to catch them with the loot. That would be the evidence we need. Something even their high-placed friends can't dismiss."

"I think we need to vet which federal agents we involve," Kate said. "Can we even trust this Boem guy? I mean, from what we've learned, we know the family connections run deep."

I slowly nodded my head, then said, "We should, if we could, but we can't. We just have to trust our gut and go with it... Hell, we don't have a choice. If it blows up in our faces... well..." I trailed off, not knowing what else to say.

I made the call to Boem and arranged a secure meeting for early the next morning and we spent the rest of the evening organizing the evidence, creating a presentation that would be acceptable to the feds. *Geez*, I thought, *never in my wildest dreams did I think I'd be cooking up a scheme like this.*

And so we all went to bed. Kate and I in my room and Sarah in the spare room. Well, Kate couldn't go back to her place, could she? That cover was blown.

But I have to tell you, sleep didn't come easy that night. My dreams were filled with men in Nazi uniforms, barbed wire fences, crematoriums billowing smoke, and hoards of stolen treasure.

As dawn broke over the Sequoya nuclear plant to the east, I stood at my window, coffee in hand, watching the river. Somewhere along its banks, one of the most audacious criminal enterprises in Tennessee history was preparing its next, and perhaps final, shipment.

13

Sunday Morning, October 21

The morning brought clear skies and a sense of momentum I hadn't felt since the investigation began. With the financial evidence secured and our federal partners on board, we finally had a plan to put this thing to bed, or so I hoped.

To placate Kate, when I met with Boem that morning, I reiterated our concerns about his people. Surprisingly, he took it well, and promised to involve only his most trusted agents.

Since, there was little more I could do or say about that and, as I had a little time on my hands, and considering the scale of what we were planning, I decided it was time to talk to Eleanor Rawlings.

I drove to the Rawlings' estate alone, leaving Kate to coordinate with Boem, and Sarah organizing and collating the evidence.

I called Eleanor and she agreed to meet me, though her response to the call had been... Well, let's say guarded. As Elizabeth's daughter-in-law, she'd been part of the family for over thirty years and seemingly involved in the families' financial affairs, but there was something odd about that, something I couldn't put my finger on, and I wanted to know what it was.

The Rawlings estate sprawled across thirty acres of prime riverfront property. The main house was a colonial revival that screamed old money.

I arrived around ten and a uniformed security guard verified my identity at the gate, then directed me to the garden rather than the house.

I found Eleanor among her roses, secateurs in hand, methodically dead-heading spent blooms. At fifty-eight, she was a strikingly beautiful woman. *A trophy wife?* I wondered.

She didn't acknowledge me immediately, finishing her work on a particularly vibrant crimson rose before setting her tools aside. But then, quite suddenly, as I approached, she stood up and turned toward me. She was dressed in denim coveralls that seemed to cover nothing of her figure but actually accentuated it, and I couldn't help but wonder if they'd been tailored especially for her. Her blonde hair was pulled back in an elegant chignon, her blue eyes sparkled, and her smile lit up her face, though I thought said smile was perhaps a little forced.

"Sergeant Starke," she said as she removed her gardening gloves and offered me her hand. "I wondered when you'd get around to me."

"I'm sorry it's taken me so long," I replied, taking her hand. "I've been following the evidence, ma'am."

The ghost of a smile crossed her face. "Just as Elizabeth predicted. Please, sit." She gestured to a wrought-iron table upon which was set a pitcher of lemonade and two glasses. "I've been expecting you since you visited the warehouse."

That stopped me cold. "You knew about that?" I asked.

"I know a great many things, Sergeant," she said as she poured lemonade into the glasses. "Including what Elizabeth was trying to accomplish with her development project."

I studied her carefully as I sat down. "You were close to her." I asked.

"Closer than most realized." Eleanor's gaze wandered across her garden. "Elizabeth was more than my mother-in-law. She was my ally in a world designed to silence women like us."

"You knew what she was investigating?" I asked as I took my recorder from my pocket. "If you don't mind, Mrs. Rawlings, I'm going to record our conversation, for the record and for your protection and mine."

"Of course," she replied, then said, "Yes, I helped her." She reached beside her chair and retrieved a weathered leather portfolio. "This collection of letters belonged to Elizabeth's sister, Charlotte. After her death, Elizabeth kept them hidden for almost forty years."

I accepted the portfolio, opening it to find dozens of letters within, their paper yellowed with age. The first was dated 1962 and addressed to "My dearest Charlotte" and signed simply "T."

"Thomas Mason," Eleanor explained. "He and Charlotte were lovers for nearly a decade, beginning in the late 1950s."

I looked up in surprise. "During the height of the family feud?" I asked.

"The family feud was… is, bullshit, Sergeant, if you'll pardon my language." She sipped her lemonade. "But what Thomas and Charlotte shared was real; perhaps the only genuine thing about that entire, elaborate charade."

I examined the letters more carefully. Thomas Mason's handwriting was elegant, his words passionate. He wrote of a future together, of breaking free from family obligations, of building something honest.

"They were planning to leave?" I asked.

Eleanor nodded. "To expose the families' criminal enterprises and escape together. Charlotte had collected evidence much like Elizabeth did: banking records, shipping manifests, photographs of both families working together while publicly feuding."

"What happened?"

"Charlotte died in a boating accident in 1968." Eleanor's voice held an old pain. "At least, that's what the official report stated, though I'm certain it wasn't an accident."

I found the last letter in the collection, dated three days before Charlotte's death. Thomas had written of a secure location where they would meet, documents they would take to the federal authorities, and their plans to disappear afterward.

"The families discovered their plan?" I said.

"Yes, and the families eliminated the threat." Eleanor corrected gently but firmly. "Just as they did with Elizabeth. Just as they've done with anyone who threatened their family business."

I studied Eleanor more carefully. There was steel beneath her cultivated exterior, and a hardness within.

"Why are you showing me this?" I asked, frowning at her.

"Because I made a promise to Elizabeth." Eleanor looked out over her garden. "She knew they would kill her if she proceeded with her plan. Charlotte had set the precedent, you see. But she firmly believed that in death, she could accomplish what Charlotte could not in life."

She paused for a moment, staring out over the meadow beyond the garden, then continued, "Elizabeth had it all, her own research, and Charlotte's. She had them dead to rights, and she knew it. She also knew they would try to stop her, but I don't think she expected them to do it where and how they did."

"And you helped her?" I asked.

"As best I could without exposing myself," she replied. "I provided access to family records, connections to witnesses, and a cover for her activities." A hint of pride entered Eleanor's voice. "My husband, James Jr., never questioned why his mother spent so much time with me. He assumed we were engaged in typical society matronly activities: charity and social events, garden club matters. You know, the activities we 'ladies' are expected to engage in." She made finger quotes close to her chest when she said 'ladies.'

"Instead, you were building a case against both families," I said.

She smiled, then nodded and said, "Yes, but it was Elizabeth that was building the case. I was merely a facilitator. After Charlotte's death, Elizabeth couldn't, wouldn't, trust anyone in either family. Except me."

"Why you?"

Eleanor's smile suggested untold secrets. "Because I had my own reasons to want the truth exposed," she replied. "My sister Mary worked for the Masons in the 1970s. She disappeared after she discovered financial irregularities in their art import business."

The pieces clicked into place. "Another victim of the family honor," I said.

"Precisely." Eleanor poured more lemonade. "Family honor; the concept they've used to justify every criminal act for three generations. Loyalty to family above all else, even basic morality."

I examined more of the letters, finding references to specific operations: valuable artifacts, meetings between family patriarchs disguised as chance encounters, profits splits.

"These letters corroborate what we found at the warehouse," I said.

Eleanor nodded and handed me a second folder. "This contains Charlotte's original documentation of the river routes used for smuggling. They still use some of them today."

The maps were detailed, showing access points, drop locations, and surveillance positions along the Tennessee and Ohio Rivers. It was at that point I realized Elizabeth had incorporated these same locations into her development plans, disguising them as construction notations.

"Elizabeth used Charlotte's research as her starting point," Eleanor explained. "Then expanded it to document the continuing operations. The development project was designed to expose the physical infrastructure while her financial investigation exposed the money trail."

"A comprehensive takedown," I said with increasing respect for the lady who'd died in my arms.

"Elizabeth understood that the families' power came from two sources, their wealth and their reputation. Her plan addressed both."

My phone buzzed. It was a text from Kate reporting that our meeting with Boem and the FBI Art Crimes team was confirmed for noon. I showed Eleanor the message.

"Be careful who you trust, Sergeant," she cautioned. "The families won't go down easily, and I can assure you they've spent decades cultivating connections within the federal agencies."

"Did Elizabeth trust the FBI Art Crimes Division?" I asked.

"Elizabeth was selective in what she shared with them." Eleanor's gaze was steady. "She understood the need for redundancies when dealing with organizations that might be compromised."

"She created multiple evidence caches?" I asked.

She shrugged. "I wouldn't be surprised if she did, but where they might be, I have no idea."

"Why are you really helping me, Mrs. Rawlings?" I asked, setting my glass down, the lemonade untouched. "You've been part of this family for decades."

"Part of, but never truly accepted," she corrected. "The inner circle of both families is bound by blood and complicity. As an in-law who never participated in their operations, I remained forever on the periphery."

"Which put you in the perfect position to observe," I said.

"Indeed." Eleanor stood, smoothing her coveralls with manicured hands. "Walk with me, Sergeant. There's something else you should see."

She led me deeper into the garden, past sculpted hedges, to a small greenhouse tucked away in a secluded corner.

The greenhouse was, in fact, a small office equipped with a desk, a filing cabinet, and a laptop computer.

"This was Elizabeth's backup office," Eleanor explained. "It's mine now. This is where we compiled evidence away from family surveillance."

The cabinet contained mostly copies of the records we'd found at the warehouse, plus some extra stuff I hadn't seen before: personnel files from the security companies, inventory lists of art pieces, shipping manifests, and more, much more.

"Elizabeth believed in redundancy," Eleanor said, as she opened a small safe hidden beneath the floorboards. "This contains hard drives with complete copies of the families' financial records, plus video evidence of family meetings where criminal operations were discussed."

I stared at the wealth of evidence. "You've been sitting on all of this while we've been investigating?"

"I've been waiting for the right moment." Eleanor's expression was unapologetic. "Elizabeth put safeguards in place," she continued. "I promised her I would only share this with someone who had already discovered enough to corroborate it independently."

"You were testing me."

"Protecting Elizabeth's work," she corrected. "If you hadn't found the warehouse, if you hadn't connected the financial dots, giving you this evidence would have been pointless. It would have been dismissed as fabricated."

She had a point. Without the trail of evidence we'd already established, a sudden information dump could have easily been discredited by the families' considerable legal resources.

"And here's something else you should know," Eleanor added, removing a final folder from the safe. "This is the information you need about tonight's shipment."

Inside was a detailed inventory of the art pieces being moved from the Mason Building vault, complete with provenance records showing their origins in collections looted during World War II. The estimated value exceeded thirty million dollars.

"How did you get this?" I asked, locking eyes with her.

"I work the family finances," she replied, holding my gaze. "And I know people, people who... well, let's just say I have a friend and leave it at that."

I checked the shipping details. "This matches what James told us."

"Be very careful, Sergeant," she said, taking my hand. "James is playing his own game." Eleanor's warning was clear. "He's not as separated from family operations as he pretends."

"You don't trust him, do you?" I asked, frowning.

"He's my son. Of course, I don't trust him," she replied, smiling bitterly. "He grew up in an atmosphere steeped in family honor. You'd be wise to remember that."

As I gathered the evidence, a question nagged at me. "Why didn't Elizabeth go public sooner? She could have. She'd been collecting evidence for years."

Eleanor's expression softened for the first time. "Because of Charlotte. Elizabeth blamed herself for her sister's death. She wanted to be absolutely certain her case was airtight before making her move."

"And the development project was the final piece," I said.

"It would have exposed the physical infrastructure of the families' enterprises while simultaneously revealing the historical evidence." Eleanor nodded. "A comprehensive revelation of facts and data that even the families' connections couldn't refute."

My phone buzzed again. It was Kate checking my status before the FBI meeting.

I showed Eleanor the message, then said, "I need to take this evidence to my partners."

"Of course," she said. "Here, take this." She handed me a business card with a number written on the back. "This is a secure line. Use it if you need to reach me. My movements will be restricted once the family realizes I've spoken with you."

I looked at her with no little concern. "Will you be safe?" I asked.

The ghost of a smile returned to her lips. "I've survived in this world for more than thirty years, Sergeant," she replied. "Thirty-six years, actually. I know how to protect myself."

As I prepared to leave, a question occurred to me. "The feud… was any of it real?"

"The hatred?" Eleanor considered. "Sometimes playacting becomes reality if practiced long enough. The families certainly competed for status, for recognition. But the core conflict was always theater, a distraction, if you will."

"And the next generation? James and Margaret?"

"They were raised on stories of family rivalry while simultaneously being groomed for collaboration." She said. "The contradiction creates a particular kind of compartmentalization. They believe the feud is real on some level, even while participating in joint operations."

"And that's why they're so effective at maintaining the deception," I said.

"Precisely. They aren't simply lying. They're living in a carefully constructed alternative reality where both the feud and the alliance coexist." She studied me carefully. "It's a form of institutional doublethink the families have perfected over three generations."

14

Sunday Morning, October 21

As I DROVE AWAY from the Rawlings estate, my mind churned as I worked through this new information. Elizabeth and Charlotte had both tried to expose the truth. Both had gathered evidence. Both had been silenced. But Elizabeth had planned for her death in ways Charlotte couldn't have.

Family honor. The concept echoed in my mind. The perceived justification for crimes spanning decades. The shield behind which two powerful families had hidden their corruption. The altar upon which Charlotte and Elizabeth had been sacrificed.

I called Kate as soon as I was clear of the estate.

"We've got a problem," I said without preamble. "I think young James might be playing both sides."

"I'm not surprised," Kate replied. "I've been doing some digging. His financial records show regular payments from a half-dozen different shell companies; all of them connected to both families."

"Eleanor Rawlings just gave me a treasure trove of new evidence," I said. "With this and what we found at the warehouse, we've got them, Kate. I'm heading your way now."

"The FBI team is standing by; their Art Crimes Division, too."

"Have Sarah vet them thoroughly," I said. "Eleanor warned me about the depth of their federal connections."

"Already on it," she replied. "So far, they appear to check out. Most of them are career investigators with solid reputations."

I merged onto the highway, checking my mirrors for tails. The security at Eleanor's gate had seen me leave, which meant both families would soon know about our meeting.

"What did Eleanor tell you about tonight's shipment?" Kate asked.

"Everything," I said, "inventory, timing, and route. Plus evidence connecting the pieces directly to Nazi looting operations."

Kate whistled softly. "The missing link between the historical crimes and current operations," she said.

"Exactly. This shipment is the smoking gun we've been looking for. I told you, Kate. We've got them."

"For their myriad crimes, yes," she said, "but not for Elizabeth's and Thorne's murders."

"I'll take what I have, party pooper," I said.

She laughed.

"See you in a minute," I said and hung up.

As I approached downtown, I spotted a black SUV slipping into the traffic behind me, the same model used by the family security teams. I took a quick right and watching as the vehicle followed.

I called Kate back. "I've picked up a tail," I told her. "I'm going to take evasive action, so it may take me a few minutes to lose them."

"Be careful, Harry," she whispered.

"Aren't I always?" I asked.

"No," she snapped.

I ended the call and focused on losing my tail. The morning traffic provided cover as I executed a series of turns designed to confirm I was being followed. The SUV stayed with me, maintaining its distance, not trying to hide their presence. *They're sending me a message?* I thought.

I took a sudden turn into the police department's parking garage, knowing they wouldn't follow me there and, as expected, the SUV cruised past. I waited several minutes, but the SUV didn't return. They were gone, but the message was clear. *They're watching me*, I thought. *Which means they know I've met with Eleanor. And that means they probably know about the evidence, too.*

I sat for a few more minutes, thinking, and then pulled out of the garage and went around the back, parked and went into the building and from there up to the conference room. It was a little after eleven-thirty.

Kate and Sarah had already prepared for the FBI meeting. They had the evidence chronologically organized, starting with the Nazi collaboration prior to Pearl Harbor and through to the present day.

"We have company," Kate said, nodding toward the conference room window. Lieutenant Marshall was watching us from across the situation room, making no effort to hide his interest.

"Eleanor was right," I muttered. "They have eyes everywhere."

"What?" Kate snapped. "Are you saying what I think you're saying, that Marshall's gone over to the dark side?"

"I wouldn't be surprised," I said, still with my eyes locked onto Marshall's.

Sarah looked worried. "D'you think we should cancel the meeting?" she asked.

"No," I replied, turning to look down at the table. "We don't have a choice. The shipment is tonight." I handed Eleanor's additional evidence to Kate and said, "better make a copy of this before they get here."

She nodded and walked over to the machine and began running the papers through it.

"We control the narrative," I said. "We decide what information we share and when."

I filled them in on my conversation with Eleanor, including her warnings about James Rawlings and possible federal infiltration.

"What about the FBI The Art Crimes team?" I asked Sarah.

"As far as I can tell, they check out," Sarah confirmed. "They've been building cases against dealers in Nazi loot for years. Agent Sam Dewer, their SAIC, told me Elizabeth contacted them directly, bypassing the usual channels."

"Smart woman," I said, echoing my earlier assessment.

As we finalized our presentation, Marshall made his move, entering the conference room without knocking.

"Quite the operation you've got here, Starke," he said, eyeing the evidence spread across the table. "Chief wants an update on the Rawlings homicide."

"I'm preparing that now," I replied evenly. "I should have it on his desk by the end of the day. Right now we're waiting for the FBI."

Marshall picked up one of the financial documents. "This looks like a lot more than a simple murder investigation."

"It's not so simple, Jack," I said, evenly. "Elizabeth Rawlings' death is connected to an ongoing criminal enterprise," I continued, taking the document from his hand. "We're pursuing all relevant leads."

"Including unauthorized warehouse searches?" he asked. "Harassment of prominent citizens?" His smile didn't reach his eyes. "The Mason and Rawlings families have filed formal complaints."

"Have they, now?" I said. "That's the first I've heard of it."

"We're conducting a thorough investigation into a homicide," Kate interjected. "Everything has been properly documented."

Marshall's attention shifted to Sarah. "And who's this? Doesn't look like department personnel to me."

"She's a civilian consultant," I said before Sarah could respond.

"Is she now? Hmm…" He paused for a few seconds, then said, "The chief will want to review all this before you share it with other agencies," Marshall said, making another attempt to examine our evidence.

"We'll brief him personally after our current meeting," I countered. "Now if you'll excuse us, Lieutenant, we have federal agents arriving momentarily."

Marshall held my gaze for a long moment before backing down. "This isn't over, Starke. The chief has serious concerns about you and your methods."

After he left, Kate closed the door. "He's definitely on their payroll," she said.

"Maybe," I said. "Or he could just be doing what the chief ordered," I said. "Either way, we need to move quickly."

The FBI team arrived moments later, Agent Boem, a senior agent named Diana Reeves, and two specialists in historical art crime. They listened attentively as we presented our evidence, connecting the financial records to specific art pieces scheduled for movement that night.

"This aligns with our own investigation," Reeves confirmed. "Elizabeth Rawlings provided similar documents linking these two families to an international network dealing in looted art."

"She was working with you?" I asked.

"For nearly a year," Reeves replied. "She contacted us after discovering financial connections between several art pieces in the Mason collection and Jewish families who lost everything during the Holocaust."

"Then why haven't you moved on it?" I asked. "She might still be alive if you had."

"It's not that simple, Harry," Boem said. "Her evidence was

good, but not conclusive. We need more. Now it looks like we have it." He looked at Reeves.

Reeves nodded. "It's the evidence we've been waiting for; physical proof connecting historical looting to present-day trafficking..." Reeves trailed off as she studied the route maps. "We need to coordinate a joint operation to intercept this shipment."

"With limited departmental involvement," I said, "yours and mine." And I explained our concerns about internal leaks.

Reeves and Boem understood immediately. "We've encountered similar issues in other jurisdictions," Reeves said. "Family influence often extends into local law enforcement."

We spent the next hour developing a plan of operation. We knew the art shipment would move from the Mason Building through what was left of the underground street system to a river access point near the old boathouse. From there, it would be transferred onto two boats heading downriver to international shipping.

"If we catch them with the art in transit, with documentation linking it to Nazi looting, we'll have an airtight case," Reeves said. "Not just against the current perpetrators; there's a possibility we could also recover pieces that have been missing since World War II."

As they prepared to leave, Reeves pulled me aside. "Elizabeth Rawlings was a remarkable woman, Sergeant. She understood the risks. You should be proud to have known her."

"Actually, I didn't know her," I replied, "not personally, though I certainly knew of her. Tell me, did she tell you she knew they were going to kill her?"

"She did," she replied, "and she certainly planned for that possibility, didn't she?" Reeves' expression was somber.

I nodded, but didn't reply. The truth is, I didn't know what to say to her. She was a senior FBI agent and, to me, an unknown quantity.

After the FBI team left, taking copies of everything with them,

Kate, Sarah, and I discussed the operational plan for that evening. We would coordinate with Reeves' team while minimizing the involvement of our department.

"What about James Rawlings?" Kate asked. "If he's playing both sides as you say, he could compromise the operation."

"We feed him only limited information," I said. "Enough to maintain his cooperation without revealing our plan. We tell him nothing about tonight's operation."

Sarah had been quiet during the FBI meeting, but now she looked troubled. "These families have maintained their criminal empire for almost seventy years. They've eliminated everyone who threatened them. What makes you think tonight will be any different?"

It was a fair question. "There are no guarantees, Sarah," I said. "We don't know who's feeding them information. It could be James. It could be Marshall, though if he knows anything, it can't be much, not unless he has my office and this conference room wired." I looked around the room, not expecting to see anything, and I didn't. "So, we just play the game and hope to win," I finished. "If you want to stay home, at my place, you're welcome."

She shook her head.

I looked at Kate. She smiled and said, "And because we know what we're up against, we're not walking in blind."

As we finalized the preparations, my thoughts returned to Eleanor's garden and the story of Charlotte and Thomas, lovers caught in the machinery of family honor, trying to break free from a system built on blood money and deception.

Family honor, I thought. *A concept that spawned three generations of crime. Well, tonight, it ends.*

15

I left Sarah scanning the original documents into her laptop, but before I did, I asked her to send them all in a file to my office desktop, then Kate and I went to my office and I pulled up Sarah's files as they came in.

I squinted at the files, my eyes burning after hours—no, days—studying decades-old reports.

"I'm going for coffee," Kate said. "You want some?"

I nodded, "Sure, black. And, Kate, make a fresh pot, please."

She smiled as she walked out the door, closing it behind her. Me? I continued scanning through the hundreds of pages, some of them so old they were difficult to read.

"Find anything?" Kate said, some fifteen minutes later. Her voice broke my concentration as she set a paper cup beside me.

"Maybe," I said, with my eyes still on the screen. "I've been going through the official reports on the 1947 mill fire. Something's off."

Kate leaned over my shoulder. "How so?"

"Look at this." I pointed to a notation in the margin of what appeared to be the original investigator's report. "The final conclusion states electrical fire, consistent with the public story. But here—" I traced my finger along a handwritten note that had been partially obscured by an official stamp. "The initial investigator, F. Sullivan, reported evidence inconsistent with an electrical fire. Those findings were not included in the final report."

Kate straightened, coffee forgotten. "Someone overruled the investigator."

"And buried his findings." I said as I scrolled through more pages, finding several sections redacted or altered in the official version. "Sullivan documented multiple ignition points and accelerant patterns."

"Professional job, do you think?" Kate asked.

"Possibly," I replied.

I continued scanning until I found a personnel file attached to the report. The photograph showed a young man in a fire marshal's uniform, his expression serious beneath his department cap.

"Frank Sullivan," I read. "He was twenty-seven at the time of the investigation. Served five years in the Army Corps of Engineers during the war. Specialty in structural fires and explosives."

"Someone with that background would recognize professional work," Kate said.

"And wouldn't mistake it for an electrical fire." I said as I scrolled further, finding a disciplinary note dated two weeks after the mill fire. "Look at this," I said. "Sullivan was reprimanded for 'pursuing unauthorized lines of inquiry' and 'making unfounded accusations against respected members of the community.'"

"The families shut him down," Kate said.

I nodded, scrolling to the last page where a handwritten note had been added to the file: *Further investigation suspended by order of Chief Marshall.*

"Marshall?" Kate's eyebrows raised. "Any relation to our lieutenant, I wonder? Geez, wouldn't that be something?"

I closed the file and pulled up Lt. Marshall's personnel file.

"His grandfather was Richard Marshall," I said, "but it doesn't say anything about what he did for a living. Coincidence, perhaps."

"Or not," Kate said, and took a sip of her coffee.

I made a note of Sullivan's name and badge number. "We need to find out if he's still alive," I muttered.

Kate was already on her phone. "I'll check the fire department pension records." After a moment, she looked up, surprised. "Frank Sullivan, retired 1990 after forty-three years of service. He's drawing a pension at a Signal Mountain address."

"Signal Mountain," I muttered. "That's an interesting location for a man on a city pension."

"Someone who kept quiet about certain findings might be receiving other forms of compensation," Kate suggested.

I stood, gathering my notes. "Elizabeth would have seen the same reports," I said

"You think she contacted Sullivan?"

"I think we need to find out what he knows." I said as I glanced at the partially redacted report one last time before closing the file and shutting down the computer. "And why someone tried to bury his findings almost sixty years ago. Come on, let's get something to eat, then go see what he has to say for himself."

It was a little after two that afternoon when I pulled into Frank Sullivan's driveway on Signal Mountain. The modest ranch house looked like thousands of others built in the 1970s: brick facade, neatly trimmed shrubs, American flag by the door. Nothing about it suggested its owner might possess information that could bring down two of Chattanooga's most powerful families.

Kate checked her watch as we approached the front door. "We've got six hours until the shipment moves," she said. "We should make this quick. I have stuff I need to get done before we go."

Sullivan, a former fire marshal who'd investigated the 1947 mill fire, was, at eighty-nine, one of the few living witnesses to the event that had launched the family feud.

A home health aide answered the door, eyeing our badges with suspicion before leading us to a sunroom where Sullivan sat in a wheelchair surrounded by banker's boxes, his gnarled hands sorting through old files.

"Sergeants Starke and Gazzara," she said as we entered the sunroom.

"I've been expecting you," he said without looking up. "Ever since Elizabeth died."

Sullivan was thinner than in the department photos I'd seen, but his eyes were sharp as he assessed us with the practiced scrutiny of a career investigator.

I took out my recorder, turned it on, set it on the side table, and said, "For the record, Mr. Sullivan, do I have your permission to record our conversation?"

He nodded. "Yeah, it's okay."

"You knew Elizabeth Rawlings?" I asked, taking a seat across from him.

"She came to see me last year," he replied. "Asked about the mill fire." He tapped a weathered folder. "She wanted to know what wasn't in the official report."

"And what was that, exactly?" Kate prompted.

Sullivan looked up, as if he was studying me carefully before making a decision. "The mill fire wasn't what they claimed. I found thermite residue. Military grade. And the vault..." He shook his head. "It was empty. But the scorch marks inside told a story. It had contained gold bars, or maybe silver; they'd been in there for years. You could see their outlines."

The old man's description matched perfectly with the financial records we'd found - evidence of gold moving through the Mason textile mill, then disappearing the night of the fire.

"Why wasn't this in your official report?" I asked.

Sullivan's laugh was sharp. "Try being a twenty-seven-year-old fire investigator accusing Chattanooga's most powerful families of arson and possibly treason. My supervisor buried my findings before the ink was dry."

"But you kept your own records," Kate noted, gesturing to the boxes surrounding him.

"Forty years in fire investigation, that's what that is," he said proudly. "Never threw away a case file." There was pride in his voice. "Created my own archive after the department 'lost' the original reports, I did."

He shuffled through one of the boxes and retrieved a folder marked simply "1947." Inside were photographs showing burn patterns consistent with accelerants, far different from the "electrical fire" described in the public accounts.

"The fire was engineered," Sullivan explained, pointing to specific patterns in the photos. "It started in multiple locations simultaneously. They were destroying evidence, so they were."

"Thermite leaves a distinctive signature," Kate noted, examining the photographs.

"The kind Rawlings Steel produced during the war," Sullivan confirmed. "Military grade. Not something civilians could easily get hold of."

"And you think both families were involved," I said, making it a statement rather than a question.

Sullivan nodded. "Security from both families was on site that night. It was a coordinated response."

He produced another photograph, black and white, grainy but clear enough to show men in Rawlings security uniforms working alongside Mason personnel loading something into trucks. "I took most of these," he said. "They took 'em all, and the negatives, so they thought, but they didn't get these."

"Three night watchmen died in that fire," Kate said softly.

"They weren't supposed to be there," Sullivan replied. "Someone changed the schedule at the last minute."

"They created necessary casualties," I muttered, remembering James Rawlings' explanation.

"And the beginning of a very public feud," Sullivan added. "A convenient distraction from their joint operation, so they say."

As he continued sharing his evidence, I noticed movement outside the front window; a black SUV cruising slowly past the house. The same model that had followed me earlier.

"Mr. Sullivan," I said, interrupting his explanation of burn patterns, "do you have security cameras on your property?"

He followed my gaze to the window. "Yeah, and motion sensors. After what happened to Elizabeth, I took precautions."

My phone buzzed. It was a text from our surveillance team leader reporting unusual activity at both family compounds. The company security teams were mobilizing again.

"That SUV," I said. "They know we're here."

Sullivan didn't seem surprised. "Been waiting sixty years for them to come and finish the job." He gestured to a metal strongbox beside his chair. "That's why I keep my insurance policy close."

The smell reached me before I saw it, and I frowned. The acrid scent of burning wood. Not visible yet, but unmistakable to anyone who'd worked homicide as long as I had.

"The back room's on fire," I shouted, rising quickly. "We need to get out of here, now!"

Kate was already on her phone calling for fire response while helping Sullivan to his feet. The health aide rushed in to help.

"Help him to the car," I said, grabbing the strongbox Sullivan had indicated.

Once outside, I could see the back of the house was already engulfed in flames, and that the fire was spreading rapidly. *This was no accident,* I thought. *Someone wants his evidence destroyed, at any cost.*

Minutes later, by the time we'd helped Sullivan down his front steps, the entire house was entirely engulfed. The file boxes —decades of meticulously preserved evidence—were gone.

"They finally came," Sullivan wheezed as we reached my car. "Been waiting sixty years. They want me dead. I know too much, don't you see? Had to keep insurance."

I hung onto the strongbox as the fire trucks came rushing up the street, sirens blasting, red lights flashing, but they were too late. By the time they were in action, Sullivan's house had been reduced almost to embers, and little more than a memory.

Sullivan watched impassively from my car as his home and a lifetime of memories were reduced to ashes. He'd waited decades for this moment, a moment he knew would be the inevitable result of his crossing the wrong people. I glanced at him through the rearview mirror, thinking he was strangely calm in the face of this life-changing loss.

"You should see a paramedic," Kate told him, obviously concerned about smoke inhalation.

"Later," he said, patting the strongbox now on his lap. "First, you need to see what I showed Elizabeth."

We drove to a nearby diner and found a corner booth away from the windows where Sullivan could recover while sharing the contents of his "insurance policy."

Inside the box were photographs showing both families together at the mill, security guards with British Sterling machine guns, the door to the underground vault, and a hand-drawn map of the tunnel system. Physical evidence that had survived decades while its keeper waited for someone to ask the right questions.

"Elizabeth came to see me last month," Sullivan explained

between sips of water. "I showed her the contents of this box. She said she was going to make it right. Poor girl didn't know. Did she? No one can make this kind of thing right. Not even you, Detectives. We can only hope to survive the knowing of it."

"The night watchmen," I said, studying reports Sullivan had preserved. "I assume they saw something they weren't supposed to see?" I asked.

Sullivan nodded grimly. "They found them checking the crates in the mill basement. Crates with Nazzy markings—" Yes, that's how he pronounced it. "They were supposed to be moving them out that night. They were not supposed to be inspected by curious night watchmen."

"So they murdered them," Kate said. "And then burned the mill and everything in it to cover it up."

"And that's when old man Mason came up with the idea of a public feud as a distraction," Sullivan added. "Masterful bit of plotting, that was. Everyone was so focused by the families' infighting, they never questioned what they'd been up to before the fire. My overlords deemed it an accident, an electrical fire. Electrical fire, my ass. The bastards used thermite, so they did, and my supervisor and his boss knew it."

My phone buzzed with another update from our surveillance team. The activity at both family estates had increased significantly. It looked like they were speeding up their timeline.

"It looks like they're on the move," I told Kate. "We need to alert Agent Reeves."

As Kate stepped away to make the call, Sullivan leaned closer to me. "Been following your career, Starke. Not afraid to ruffle a few feathers when necessary, are you, son?"

"Comes with the job, Frank," I replied

"Including stepping on Bull Marshall's toes?" Sullivan's eyes held a knowing gleam and his lips a toothy smile.

I frowned. "Marshall?" I asked. "What about him?"

"That man's been in the families' pocket for years," he said.

That caught my attention. "You have evidence of that?" I asked.

Sullivan opened the strongbox and removed a thin manila file. "Marshall worked security for the Masons in the late '90s, before joining the police. He handled what they called 'special projects' for them, like evidence disposal, witness intimidation. You know, the usual heavy stuff. Look at these."

He handed me several photographs showing a younger Jack Marshall meeting with Thomas Mason, exchanging documents in what appeared to be the warehouse we'd visited.

"He's been their plant in the PD for almost two decades," Sullivan said. "Rising through the ranks. Protecting the family interests."

The pieces clicked into place. It all made sense.

"Why are you showing me this?" I asked, though I already knew the answer.

"Because you're going to need it." Sullivan's assessment was clinical. "A man like that won't go down easy."

As Kate returned, Sullivan closed the strongbox. "The wheel turns," he said philosophically. "The fire at the mill. The fire at my house. It's what they call karma, I suppose."

"You're remarkably calm about losing your home," Kate said.

"Been expecting it for a long, long time." Sullivan's acceptance of his situation was absolute. "It's the price of knowing what I know."

My phone rang. It was Johnston.

"Chief?" I said, frowning

"I need you back here now, Harry," he snapped and hung up without waiting for an answer.

"We've got a problem," I told Kate as I put my phone back in my pocket. "The chief wants us back at the station."

"Now?" she asked, wide eyed. "With the operation only hours away?"

"I think Marshall must be making his move," I said, showing

her Sullivan's file. "He's been working for the families since before he joined the force."

Sullivan insisted on coming with us. "I'm not staying anywhere alone," he said. "They'll just come and finish what they started."

We arranged for a patrol unit to transport him to a secure medical facility—one not controlled by either family—while Kate and I headed back to the PD.

THE CHASE
Sunday, October 21, 1pm

WE ENTERED the chief's office to find Lieutenant Marshall already there, a sly, satisfied smile on his face.

"Here they are," he announced. "Our rogue detectives."

Johnston looked tired; the political pressures of his position evidenced by the lines around his eyes. "Sergeant Starke, Sergeant Gazzara. I understand you've been conducting unauthorized operations against the Mason and Rawlings families."

"We're investigating Elizabeth Rawlings' murder," I replied evenly. "But you know that, Chief, seeing as you authorized it. We've been following lines of enquiry that connect both families to historical crimes and ongoing criminal enterprises."

"Without proper departmental authorization," Marshall interjected. "Harassing prominent citizens without probable cause, breaking into private property, interfering with a federally protected historical site."

I met the chief's gaze directly. "Sir," I said. "We have evidence connecting both families to Nazi collaboration during World War II, followed by decades of criminal activity and, possibly, the murders of Elizabeth Rawlings and Robert Thorne."

"That's quite an accusation, Sergeant." The chief's tone was carefully neutral.

"We have documentation," Kate added. "Financial records, shipping manifests, physical evidence recovered from multiple locations."

"Including a warehouse you entered illegally," Marshall countered.

"We had probable cause connecting it to Elizabeth Rawlings' murder," I said. "And we've since coordinated with federal authorities who have jurisdiction over the historical crimes."

The chief's interest sharpened. "Which federal authorities?"

"FBI Art Crimes Division," Kate replied. "They've been building a case against an international network trafficking in Nazi-looted art. Elizabeth Rawlings was their confidential informant and that, we think, was the motive for her murder."

Marshall's expression tightened almost imperceptibly. This was information he hadn't anticipated.

"We have a joint operation planned for this evening," I continued, watching Marshall carefully. "To intercept a shipment of looted artifacts being moved through the families' smuggling infrastructure."

"This is the first I'm hearing of any joint operation," the chief said, frowning.

"That's due to…" I paused, looking pointedly at him.

"We think there's a departmental leak, Chief," Kate explained diplomatically. "The families have extensive connections."

Marshall scoffed. "These are just conspiracy theories to justify their cowboy tactics."

I removed Sullivan's file from my jacket. "Actually, we have documentation of those connections, Chief." I placed the file on his desk, open to the photographs of Marshall with Thomas

Mason. "Including Lieutenant Marshall's long-standing relationship with the Mason family."

It felt like the temperature in the room dropped ten degrees. Marshall's face flushed dark red as the chief examined the photographs.

"This is a setup," Marshall sputtered. "Fabricated evidence."

"Taken by Fire Marshal Frank Sullivan in 1998," I countered. "It's part of an independent investigation he maintained after the department buried his findings on the 1947 mill fire."

The chief closed the file slowly. "Jack, I think you should wait outside."

"Chief, you can't possibly—" Marshall began, but the chief cut him off.

"Outside, Lieutenant Marshall, now." Johnston's tone left no room for argument.

After Marshall stalked out, the chief leaned back in his chair. "You just put me in one hell of a position, Harry."

"That was not my intention, sir."

"Never is." He sighed and rubbed his temples. "Tell me about this operation tonight."

We laid out the plan. "We're coordinating with FBI Art Crimes to intercept the shipment as it emerges from the tunnel system connected to the Underground," I began. "The plan is to capture both the stolen artifacts and the evidence connecting them to Nazi looting operations."

"And you believe this will provide sufficient evidence to prosecute both families?"

"For current crimes, yes," Kate confirmed. "The historical evidence may be more complicated because of the statute of limitations, but the ongoing criminal enterprise falls well within our prosecutorial reach."

The chief considered this. "And Marshall's involvement?" he asked.

"Sullivan's evidence suggests he's been protecting family

interests within the department for years," I said. "Including interfering with our current investigation."

Johnston nodded slowly. "I must admit, I've had concerns about Jack's connections for some time. I've had nothing concrete to act on, though."

"Until now," Kate added.

The chief made his decision. "You have departmental authorization for tonight's operation. Minimum personnel, your selection only. I want this done by the book, Harry. I want there to be no room for legal challenges."

"And Marshall?" I asked.

"I'll handle the Lieutenant." Johnston's expression was grim. "He'll be occupied with administrative matters until further notice."

When we left the chief's office, we found Marshall waiting in the hallway, his fury barely contained.

"You're making a big mistake, Starke," he growled. "These families have long memories."

"So do I," I replied, stopping to face him. "And I remember every case you've interfered with, every investigation you've obstructed, every time you've protected criminals instead of serving this department."

"You think you've won?" Marshall's laugh was ugly. "You have no idea what you're up against."

"Actually, I do," I said as I held his gaze. "But that ends tonight."

Marshall stepped closer, lowering his voice. "You'll never make it to tonight's operation. Accidents happen, Starke. Even to cops who think they're untouchable."

"Is that a threat, Lieutenant?"

"It's a reality check," he said as he drew back his massive shoulders and straightened his tie. "The families protected Elizabeth for decades before deciding she'd become a liability. What makes you think you'll fare any better?"

Kate stepped between us. "We made copies of everything, Marshall, and we distributed them to multiple agencies. The families are done, and so are you. If anything happens to either of us, it will be only a matter of time before they track you down. And if nothing happens to us... well, we'll just have to see, won't we?"

Something in her tone gave him pause. The calculation was visible in his eyes. The man was weighing options, assessing the risks.

"The chief may have bought your story for now," he said finally. "But this isn't over."

"For you, it is," I replied. "Sullivan's evidence is damning. Your career is finished."

Marshall's expression hardened. "We'll see about that," he snapped.

As he stalked away, Kate turned to me. "Harry, I think we may have pushed him a little too far. I'd bet my pension he's on his way to warn them."

"I'm counting on it," I said.

She looked at me, her eyebrows raised in question.

"Psychology," I said. "The more pressure we put on the families, the more likely they are to make mistakes. They've operated unchallenged for so long, they don't know how to handle real opposition."

We spent the next hour finalizing our preparations for the evening's operation. Sarah Walker was to travel in the van with the surveillance team; Kate and I in my unmarked car.

"SULLIVAN'S TUNNEL maps match what we've found," she said, poring over the map. "It looks like the access point near the old boathouse, here," she pointed and continued, "is still in use. I think it's most likely they'll emerge there and then transfer the shipment onto a boat, here." She pointed to a nearby boat dock.

Agent Reeves nodded, issued the orders and then waited for confirmation that her team was in position.

"They're here," I said to Sarah after receiving a short text. "You'd better go."

She nodded, gathering up her things, and I had a uniformed officer conduct her through the situation room and down to the waiting van.

She was to aid in establishing visual and digital surveillance at a key, but secluded, point above what we assumed would be the exit point near the boat dock. With the chief's authorization, we'd selected a small team of officers we personally trusted, briefing them on the absolute minimum they needed to know.

As evening approached, I checked in with the medical facility where Sullivan had been taken. His condition had deteriorated. Smoke inhalation compounded by his age and pre-existing conditions had done what the combined might of the two families could not.

"He's asking for you," the doctor told me. "Says he has something else to share before it's too late."

"We don't have time," Kate said when I relayed this to her. "The shipment moves in less than two hours."

"I'll make time," I said. "You coordinate the final preparations. I'll go see Sullivan and then I'll join you at the staging area."

The medical facility was quiet, a plain-clothed officer was discreetly positioned outside Sullivan's door, another at the end of the hall. They were both officers I knew personally, not department-assigned.

The old fire marshal looked frailer than he had just hours earlier. He wasn't on a ventilator, but he was receiving oxygen to assist his labored breathing.

"Didn't think it would hit me this hard," he wheezed as I entered. "Getting old's a bitch."

"You wanted to see me, Frank?"

Sullivan nodded weakly. "One last thing you need to know." He gestured for me to come closer. "I would have told you before, but the fire…" He trailed off, coughed, then continued. "The night watchmen. They weren't just random employees. All three were Mason men. That's why they were checking shipments they should've ignored."

I frowned. "So?" I said.

"One was Stacy Mason, Thomas Mason's illegitimate son." Sullivan's revelation was followed by a coughing fit. "The boy had suspicions about his father's business, and he wasn't happy, so he started investigating on his own."

"How d'you know this?" I asked.

"He came to me later that night and told me about his suspicions," Sullivan replied.

"So it wasn't just about the shipments," I said. "It was personal."

"Family business," Sullivan confirmed. "Always comes back to blood, don't it?"

"And Stacy Mason knew what he was doing?" I asked. "What about the Rawlings?"

"Yes, Mason knew," he replied. "Rawlings found out later." Sullivan's breathing grew more labored. "That's why the feud started for real. Rawlings was furious about being kept in the dark. About having to share responsibility for killing Mason's son."

"So some of the hatred between the families was genuine."

"Oh yeah. It started as BS, evolved into something real, then devolved back again." Sullivan managed a weak smile. "Life imitating art," he wheezed.

His condition worsened suddenly, monitors began beeping, the medical staff rushed in and I was ushered out as they worked to stabilize him.

I went away thinking his revelation had added yet another layer to the families' complex relationship.

By the time I reached my car, Kate was calling with an urgent update.

"Marshall's gone off-grid," she reported. "He left right after your confrontation. His phone's turned off, and he's not at any of his usual locations."

"He's warning the families," I said, starting the engine. "Or worse."

"The FBI is tapping the families' cell phone transmissions," Sarah interjected from the moving van. "They've moved it up. They're moving it now."

I checked my watch. They were moving nearly two hours earlier than planned.

"Does Reeves know?" I asked. "I'm heading to the staging area." I didn't wait for an answer because, as I pulled onto Highway 27, I noticed a vehicle following closely, a department-issued Crown Victoria with tinted windows. No light bar, no visible markings, but I recognized the silhouette behind the wheel. It was Marshall.

Geez, I thought. *Wouldn't you know it? He's not just warning the families. He's trying to make sure I never reach the operation. Well, we'll frickin' see.*

The Crown Vic sped up and rammed my rear bumper with enough force to make me swerve. The crazy SOB was trying to make it look like an accident on the busy highway. "Two can play that game, asshole!" I muttered.

I regained control and assessed my options as Marshall prepared for another strike. But the irony of it wasn't lost on me. After bringing down two of Chattanooga's most powerful families, I might be taken out by a corrupt cop with a personal grudge.

Marshall's second attempt came as we approached the Ridge Cut, a notoriously dangerous stretch of highway with steep drops on either side. His Crown Vic pulled alongside mine, then swerved sharply into my lane, forcing me toward the guardrail.

I braked hard, dropping behind him, then sped up again. The dance continued for nearly a mile, Marshall trying to force me off the road while I evaded his increasingly desperate maneuvers.

Then I spotted an opening, a gap in the traffic that would let me reach the upcoming exit. I accelerated hard, pulling alongside Marshall's vehicle. For a moment, our eyes met through the side windows, his filled with hate. Me? I smiled at him, knowing it would enrage him even further, and I was right. He made a mistake.

Marshall swerved again, but this time I was ready for him. I braked just enough so that his maneuver carried him past me. Then, the momentum of his failed attack and the pit maneuver I executed sent his Crown Vic into an uncontrolled slide. I watched in my rearview mirror as he over-corrected, the vehicle spinning across the lanes before crashing into the concrete median.

I didn't stop. Marshall had made his choice, and I had an operation to save. Kate answered on the first ring.

"Marshall just tried to run me off the road," I said, taking the exit toward our staging area. "He's wrecked, and he's down against the median on I-24 westbound just beyond the 4th Avenue exit, but I don't know for how long."

"I'll send officers to secure him," she replied. "But, Harry, the shipment's already moving. Reeves' team is in position, but they need us now."

I looked at the clock on the dash. It was just after seven. "I'm on my way," I said as I stamped on the gas pedal, leaving Marshall and his wrecked vehicle behind. "Tell Reeves to hold until I arrive. We'll get only one shot at this."

Night was falling fast. The sun had already set over Lookout Mountain as I raced toward the river. Somewhere in the shadows of Chattanooga's riverfront, a shipment of artifacts looted during

World War II was moving through the infrastructure built on Nazi gold. And, once again, I couldn't help but think how Elizabeth Rawlings had died, and how Robert Thorne and Frank Sullivan had lost everything, documenting the pattern of evil that connected the past to the present. And that now it was my job... our job, to finish what they'd started, to bring down an empire built on blood money and family honor. And it was made worse by the smell of smoke that still lingered in my clothes as I drove. The families had used fire to hide their secrets in 1947, and again today at Sullivan's house. *Damn them*, I thought savagely. *Well, they can't burn the truth.*

As I approached the staging area where Kate, Reeves and the surveillance van waited, I thought of what Sullivan had said, that the faux family feud had evolved into genuine hatred over Mason's son's death.

Family honor, I thought. *The concept that justified every crime committed over three generations. Well, tonight... it ends.*

17

Sunday, October 21, 8pm

Night had fallen completely by the time I reached our staging area - a maintenance facility half a mile from the river access point where the shipment would emerge. I smiled at Kate's obvious relief as I pulled in alongside the unmarked FBI vehicles.

"Cutting it close, weren't you?" she asked as I joined her and Agent Reeves beside a tactical van.

"But I made it, didn't I?" I said and gave her a quick hug. "What about Marshall?"

"The state police have him in custody," she replied as I checked my weapon and radio. "He claimed it was a simple traffic incident gone wrong. But a call to the chief was all it took. He's on his way to the station now."

Reeves spread a half-dozen surveillance photos across the hood of the van. "The shipment's already on the move," she said. "I only hope we've got this right. If we have, we should see them emerge any minute now. If not..." she shrugged as she trailed off.

Inside the vans, the screens displayed feeds from infrared

thermal imaging cameras positioned along the river. FBI agents in tactical gear made final preparations while our small contingent of trusted officers secured the perimeter.

"If that's true," Kate said, checking her watch, "they're twenty minutes earlier than our updated timeline. Marshall must have been able to warn them."

"Which means they know we're onto them," I said. "But they don't know about Sullivan's maps or how much of their route has been compromised."

Sarah Walker's voice came through our comms from inside the van. "The thermal imaging cameras are picking up four individuals at the exit point, but they're not moving."

"They must be waiting for the shipment," Reeves said, then outlined how she wanted to handle it. "We let them emerge with the shipment," she said as she looked around at the assembled agents. "We need them out in the open with the artifacts before we make our move. I want that on camera. The chain of evidence has to be unbreakable."

And so the countdown began, and we waited, watching the exit point. Through my night-vision binoculars, I watched the seemingly abandoned boathouse where Elizabeth had found her evidence.

"Something's happening," Kate whispered. "The four at the exit point are..." She trailed off as the boathouse door opened, and two men emerged to scan the area. Seemingly satisfied, one of them turned and signaled to someone inside.

"I think they're here," Reeves said. "Nobody move. Everyone hold your positions."

Three more men exited the boat house, followed by what we'd been waiting for: four more men, then four more, all with two-wheelers carrying crates. Even from our position, through my binoculars, I could see they were museum-quality packages.

"Ma'am—" one of the senior agents began, but Reeves cut him off.

"Hold your positions," she snapped. "We wait for the buyers."

I studied the scene. Something was nagging at me. "Where are the family representatives?" I muttered.

Then, as if on cue, a black Mercedes pulled up to the boathouse and James Rawlings III stepped out, followed by Margaret Mason. *And there it is,* I thought. *I was right. Young James was playing us.*

"There's our missing piece," Kate whispered. "The third-generation family leadership is overseeing the operation."

And then something else caught my attention. A second vehicle was approaching from the opposite direction. *The buyer, presumably,* I thought, but then, as it drew closer, I recognized Thomas Mason in the passenger seat, with James Rawlings Jr. driving.

"Oh my. It looks like the patriarchs are here too," I said, focusing my binoculars.

"Our sources indicated this was to be their last shipment before shutting down operations," Reeves said. "They're obviously clearing things up."

The families' four leaders converged at the boat house together as the security team continued unloading crates.

"We need to move," I said to Reeves. "They're preparing to scatter."

"Not until the buyer makes contact. We need the complete transaction."

Only minutes later, a third vehicle approached, a Bentley, that stopped at a discreet distance, and two men emerged.

"The tall one is Heinrich Schröder," Sarah's voice said into our ears. "He's a German national with connections to an international network of art dealers. Interpol has been after him for years."

And, so it seemed, the pieces were indeed finally falling into place: the sellers, the buyers, the looted artifacts, all present and all captured on multiple surveillance systems, and I couldn't help but smile to myself.

"Wait for my mark," Reeves instructed as Schröder approached the assembled group.

The security teams had arranged the crates for inspection. James Rawlings III opened one, revealing an ornately framed painting wrapped in protective material. Even from our distance, the surveillance cameras captured enough detail for Sarah to confirm its identity.

"That's 'Woman in Gold,' variation by Klimt," she said. "It's been documented as having been seized from the Blumenthal collection in Vienna, 1938. It's officially listed as destroyed during the war."

"We have positive identification of a looted artifact," Reeves confirmed. "Let's take 'em down. Go! Go! Go!"

The operation unfolded smoothly and with precision. FBI agents emerged from concealed positions all around the boathouse, weapons drawn, while our officers secured the perimeter.

Agent Reeves rushed forward, bullhorn in hand, shouting instructions to the surprised criminals.

The family security people reacted professionally, raising their hands in the face of overwhelming force and complying immediately with Reeves' instructions to get on the ground.

I smiled as I watched the varying reactions of the family members. James Rawlings III and Margaret Mason seemed almost relieved, while the patriarchs maintained the stoic, dignified composure of men long accustomed to legal challenges.

I stood by as Reeves read the federal charges, a comprehensive list of felonies spanning arts theft, money laundering, tax evasion, wire fraud and RICO violations.

I waited until she'd finished, then took my turn. "Thomas Mason. James Rawlings Jr., you're also under arrest for conspiracy to commit murder in the deaths of Elizabeth Rawlings and Robert Thorne, and the attempted murder of Frank Sullivan." Sullivan was a bit of a stretch, but seeing as the fire at his home had been deliberately set, I thought I'd throw it in for good measure. And then I read them their rights.

Thomas Mason's composure cracked slightly. "You have no evidence connecting us to any of those unfortunate events."

"Actually, I think we do," I said benignly. "We have financial records detailing payments to the security team that carried out the hit on Elizabeth Rawlings. Eleanor Rawlings has provided us with quite a comprehensive package. And we have witnesses that will testify it was one of your teams that carried out the search of Thorne's office and his subsequent murder. And with what these people are facing," I waved my hand at the now secured private security officers, "I'm sure one or more of them will want to cut a deal."

At the mention of Eleanor, James Rawlings Jr. finally showed emotion—genuine surprise. "Eleanor? Impossible," he said. "She's been loyal to the family for forty years."

"To Elizabeth, yes," I corrected him. "Not to the criminal enterprise you disguised as family business. As crime families go, you two must rank near the top."

As our officers secured the prisoners, Reeves supervised the documentation of the artifacts. Each crate was photographed and its contents carefully cataloged before being transferred to the FBI transport.

"Seventeen pieces," Reeves reported. "All matching Elizabeth Rawling's inventory of Nazi-looted art."

"Plus the financial documentation Eleanor provided connecting them directly to the original thefts," I added, watching as her agents cataloged and photographed a number of hard drives and documents from James Rawlings III's briefcase.

The young family leader had surrendered his materials without resistance. "It was always going to end this way," he said as I approached him, shaking my head.

"It was, James," I said, "but you had your chance to step away. What happened?"

"I cooperated because I was trying to salvage what I could." There was no remorse in his admission. "I was playing both sides, trying to ensure my own survival."

"While setting us up to walk into an ambush tonight." At his surprised look, I continued. "The timeline change wasn't just because of Marshall's warning, was it? You fed us misinformation from the beginning, didn't you?"

"Family loyalty still counts for something, Sergeant."

"Enough to protect murderers?" I asked. "You do know you're complicit in those murders?"

He shrugged. "I understand that some legacies are complicated." He glanced toward the artwork being loaded into FBI secure transport. "Those pieces were always going to be returned to their rightful owners," he said. "Elizabeth had arranged it months ago."

"What are you talking about?"

"Oh come on, Harry," he said, smiling at me. "Why do you think she documented everything so thoroughly? The provenance, the chain of custody, the connections to the original owners?" James shook his head. "She wasn't just building a criminal case. She was creating the paper trail necessary for restitution."

I wasn't stunned by the revelation, but I was taken aback. To learn Elizabeth hadn't just been working to expose the criminal enterprise, that she'd been systematically documenting the looted art so it could be returned to the descendants of those who had lost everything during the Holocaust, it provided insight into just what kind of a woman she really was.

I think James could tell what I was thinking because he smiled and said, "Grandmother Elizabeth was nothing if not thorough. I guess I'll see you in court, Harry," he said as they led him away toward a transport vehicle.

"Oh, you'll see me before then," I called after him.

As the scene was secured, I joined Kate and Reeves at the command van where Sarah was helping process the evidence.

The operation continued into the early morning hours as the FBI secured additional evidence from the boathouse and sealed the tunnel entrance.

Among the records taken from the boathouse were dossiers on each family member's involvement, including those who'd been kept on the periphery. Eleanor Rawlings featured prominently, her perceived loyalty documented alongside notes about keeping her "usefully uninformed."

"They never suspected she was working with Elizabeth," Kate said as she reviewed the files. "Their arrogance blinded them."

It was almost dawn when we finally concluded the on-site operation. The artifacts were transported to a secure federal facility, the evidence cataloged, photographed and processed according to strict chain-of-custody protocols.

"We've barely scratched the surface," Reeves told me as her team prepared to depart. "The financial details will take months to unravel."

"But you have what you need for the immediate charges?" I asked.

"More than enough," she replied. "The RICO case is airtight. Money laundering, art theft, tax evasion, wire fraud - multiple federal violations spanning decades," she said as she shook my hand. "It's an extraordinary case."

As the federal teams departed, Kate and I remained at the site, watching the sunrise over the Tennessee River. The same waters that had carried Nazi gold seventy years earlier had witnessed the end of the criminal empire built upon that blood money.

"It's hard to believe it's over," Kate said, leaning against my car.

"Thanks to Elizabeth," I replied.

"And it cost her her life," Kate whispered.

"It was a price she was prepared to pay." I said.

I thought of Sullivan's revelation about the night watchmen, about Thomas Mason's illegitimate son dying in a fire designed to protect family secrets.

"Everything circles back to misguided family honor," I muttered.

We drove to the hospital where Sullivan had been taken, only to learn he'd passed away during the night. The nurse who had cared for him handed me an envelope.

"He asked me to give you this if you came back," she said. "Said it was the final piece of the puzzle."

Inside was a photograph I hadn't seen before, a group portrait dated September 1946 showing the Rawlings and Mason families together with a number of wealthy-looking people. Standing among them was a young man whose resemblance to Thomas Mason was unmistakable.

"The illegitimate son," Kate said, examining the image. "Working at the mill."

I turned the photograph over. Written on the back in Sullivan's shaky hand: *Thomas Stacy Mason Jr. who died in the mill fire set by his own father.*

The chief was waiting when we returned to the station, his expression a mixture of exhaustion and grim satisfaction.

"Quite a night, Sergeants," he said. "How are you feeling?"

"Tired," I said. Kate said nothing.

"Tired?" Johnston repeated. "Is that all you can say? I thought you'd be elated at the result."

"Yeah, well, maybe when we've had some sleep," I said, dryly.

"Before you go," he said, gesturing to the conference room where Lieutenant Marshall sat with two department attorneys. "Your former colleague is negotiating a deal in exchange for information about his involvement with the families."

"How generous of him," I said.

"Self-preservation." The chief said, shaking his head. "Twenty years on the force, and his true loyalty was always elsewhere."

"So, what happens now?" Kate asked.

"For Marshall? Depends on what he gives us. For the families? Federal prosecution will handle the criminal charges. Civil proceedings will determine restitution for the looted art." He studied me carefully. "For you two, there's still Elizabeth Rawlings' murder to officially close."

"It's… complicated," Kate said, "but we think we have the evidence connecting the patriarchs to the security team that carried out the hit."

"Then finish your report. By the book." His emphasis was clear. "This case is sure to be scrutinized for years to come."

It was seven-thirty that morning when we left to go home to shower and get a few hours sleep, four, to be precise.

GUT FEELINGS
   Monday, October 22, 2:30pm

IT WAS JUST after two-thirty when we arrived back at the office, refreshed but still weary. The enormity of what we'd achieved had still not set in.

We were greeted by congratulatory hand-shakes all round and then we settled in and spent the rest of the day completing our reports. We were able to connect Elizabeth's and Robert Thorne's murders to the broader criminal enterprise we'd exposed, but whether or not it would stand up in court…? To be perfectly honest, I wasn't entirely sure. The evidence was comprehensive. The financial records of payments to the security team were solid enough. But the communications ordering the hit were disguised as business correspondence. We also had a witness statement from Eleanor Rawlings, but was it enough? I still wasn't sure. What we really needed was to turn James Rawlings III, but could we?

"I wonder how she felt?" I said.

"Who?" Kate asked.

"Elizabeth. I wonder how she felt knowing they would kill her to keep her quiet," I said as we finalized our report.

"I think she was up for it," Kate replied. "She was one tough lady, that's for sure. Hell, Harry, she turned her own murder into a trap."

Sarah Walker joined us late that afternoon, bringing news from her father's medical facility.

"Dad's being released tomorrow," she reported. "His doctors say he's recovered enough to continue rehabilitation at home."

"And then?" Kate asked.

"There's still work to do helping identify all the artifacts and their rightful owners." She replied, smiling. "Elizabeth would have wanted us to see it through, I think."

And then we received another surprise. As evening approached, we received word that Eleanor Rawlings had called a press conference. We watched from the PD as she addressed the gathered media with the poise of someone accustomed to public scrutiny.

"Three generations ago," she began, "my husband's family entered into an arrangement that began with collaboration with Nazi Germany and evolved into decades of criminal activity," she stated calmly. "This was disguised behind a theatrical feud with the Mason family, while both families actually worked together to maintain their criminal enterprises."

The reporters erupted with questions, but Eleanor continued steadily.

"Elizabeth Rawlings discovered this deception and spent years documenting it, working with federal authorities to build a case that would not only expose the crimes but ensure restitution for those who lost their priceless cultural heritage during the Holocaust."

She outlined the basic facts of the case, the Nazi collaboration, the mill fire, the decades of smuggling disguised by the fake feud, with the calm demeanor of someone who had waited decades to speak these truths.

"Elizabeth paid for her commitment to justice with her life," Eleanor concluded. "But she ensured the truth would survive her. The artifacts recovered last night will be returned to the descendants of their rightful owners. The financial proceeds of these criminal enterprises will be subject to federal forfeiture. And those responsible will face justice after decades of impunity."

It was later that evening, and Kate and I were home when my phone rang. It was Eleanor.

"So, did you see it, Harry?"

"I did. It was quite a performance," I said.

"Not a performance, Harry," she said. "Not anymore."

"So, what happens to you now?" I asked.

"I'll cooperate with federal prosecutors, provide testimony where needed, and then…" She paused. "Charlotte had a daughter. She was raised by relatives after her death. Elizabeth located her years ago but never made contact, fearing it would put her at risk. I think it's time she learned who her mother really was."

We talked for a few moments more before she ended the call saying, "If there's ever anything I can do for you, Harry, you only have to ask."

I thanked her and she ended the call. Kate and I stood at the window overlooking the river. The lights on the Thrasher Bridge glimmered on the dark waters of the Tennessee.

"How many lives were damaged to protect their secrets, d'you think?" Kate mused, my arm around her waist, her head on my shoulder.

"Too many," I said as I thought of Sullivan, of Charlotte, of Elizabeth, of Mason's son, Thorne, and the three night watchmen, all lives consumed by the machinery of family power. "But now it's over."

My phone buzzed. It was a text from Reeves with an update from federal prosecutors. Formal charges were being prepared and would be filed against the principal members of both families, the patriarchs and James III and Margaret Mason.

I shook my head, knowing the investigation would continue for months, possibly years and, because of who they were, they'd probably be granted bail, especially as most of their crimes were covered by the statute of limitations. Yes, they were in possession of stolen artifacts, which was indeed a crime, but the financial dealings spanning decades, the properties acquired through criminal proceeds, artifacts still missing from collections lost during the war, those were, to me at least, going to be iffy to prove. Only the murders were outside the statute of limitations, and those, being state crimes, were up to us to prove and charge. Fortunately, we had Elizabeth's meticulous documentation and Eleanor's and Sullivan's evidence that would provide motives for the murders. But, in my opinion, it was still going to be an uphill battle.

"What about Marshall?" Kate asked.

"Federal custody," I replied. "Singing like a canary, apparently, about departmental interference over the years. The chief's ordered a complete review of every case Marshall touched."

"That's going to keep Internal Affairs busy for a while," she said. "But good. We might actually find some cases worth reopening."

The night had deepened and the traffic on the bridge slowed, and the weight of the events of the past week settled heavily on my shoulders.

I released Kate, turned her around, pulled her to me, and kissed her gently, holding the kiss for many seconds before releasing her.

"What was that for?" she whispered.

"I dunno," I said. "It scratched an itch, I suppose."

Outside, the moon came from behind a cloud and the Tennessee turned into a river of molten silver.

"It started with blood money," I said.

"And it ends with restitution," Kate replied.

I nodded. "The legacy of lies that sustained two of Chattanooga's most powerful families has finally crumbled," I muttered, "exposed by an old woman whose commitment to truth was unbreakable, even in the face of death."

"It was all about family honor and pride," Kate said.

"And ultimately that's what brought them down," I said.

"Let's go to bed, Harry," she whispered.

And we did, but somewhere deep down in my gut, I had a feeling we hadn't yet seen the end of it.

And I was right.

[illegible] with [illegible] affirmation of the [illegible]

[illegible] [illegible] that [illegible] two of [illegible] [illegible] family [illegible] [illegible] [illegible] by [illegible] whose [illegible] to [illegible] was unreasonable [illegible] of death."

"It was all about family honor and pride," [illegible] said.

"And [illegible] that's what brought them [illegible]," I said.

"[illegible] got [illegible] right [illegible]."

[illegible]

[illegible] [illegible] of [illegible]

And I was right.

19

ECHOES OF '47
Monday, October 29

The week after the arrests passed in a blur of paperwork, interviews, and evidence processing. Each interrogation brought new revelations. Each document we reviewed added layers to the families' decades-long deception. The scale of their operation exceeded even our estimates: properties throughout the Southeast, political connections stretching to Washington and beyond, financial tentacles extending into legitimate businesses across multiple states and countries.

It was Monday morning, and I arrived in my office at eight to find the sunlight streaming through the window. I stood for a moment, then got to work reviewing the latest findings. The pattern of recent fires across Chattanooga had finally clicked into place. Each blaze targeting a building where evidence from 1947 might still exist. The families' security teams had been systematically destroying records, following a playbook established after the original mill fire.

"You look like you haven't slept," Kate said, as she entered with coffee in hand.

"I've been working through Sullivan's stuff." I said, accepting the cup gratefully. "He documented similar fire patterns after previous threats to family operations. It's always been their preferred method for eliminating evidence."

Kate pulled up a chair. "The fire department completed their analysis of Sullivan's house. It was arson. They used a small, military-grade thermite grenade."

"The signature Rawlings Steel product," I nodded.

"A family recipe," Kate replied, with a hint of humor.

The intercom buzzed. Sarah Walker had arrived with her father. I looked at my watch. It was five after nine. Dr. Walker had been released from the hospital the day before. His recovery was progressing, but he still required a wheelchair and oxygen. His determination to contribute to the investigation had overruled his doctors' recommendations for extended rest.

"I feel obligated to see it through," Walker explained after Sarah had wheeled him into my office. "Elizabeth would have wanted it so."

His color was better than when I'd last seen him, though the bullet wound, and subsequent complications had taken a visible toll. His academic intellect, however, remained undiminished.

He leaned forward in the wheelchair and spread some of his research materials across my desk.

"I've been analyzing the security personnel records," he said, his voice slightly breathless despite the oxygen. "Both families maintained private security companies that worked together even prior to 1947. Those companies are still being run by the families to this day."

I looked at the documents. They showed employment records spanning three generations.

"Institutional knowledge," Kate noted.

"Precisely." Walker pointed to specific names. "Many of these men have been with the families since their late teens. Their loyalty wasn't just purchased... Well, it was, but it was also cultivated through generations of interdependence."

My cell phone rang. It was Chief Johnston requesting an update. I stepped out to take the call while Kate and the Walkers continued reviewing the security records.

"Harry, the federal prosecutor needs your final report," Johnston said without preamble. "The grand jury convenes next week."

"We're wrapping everything up today," I assured him. "I'm finalizing the connections between the historical crimes and current operations."

"And Marshall?"

"His testimony corroborates the pattern of departmental interference," I confirmed.

The chief's sigh carried through the phone. "It's a mess, Harry. IA's preliminary review suggests at least thirty cases were compromised. We'll be untangling this mess for years."

"Any word on his plea deal?"

"Federal witness protection in exchange for his testimony," Johnston said, bitterly. "He'll disappear after the grand jury."

The chief's tone made clear his disgust at the arrangement, but we both understood the necessity. Marshall's testimony would help secure convictions against much bigger fish.

The conversation continued for a couple of minutes more, then the chief abruptly ended the call with an admonishment, "Don't let me down, Harry."

I shook my head and returned to my office to find the Walkers had arranged the security records chronologically, revealing a pattern that matched Sullivan's documentation of suspicious fires.

"Every time someone threatened to expose the families, fires eliminated evidence in the same pattern," Sarah explained, highlighting dates. "1947, 1968, 1985, and now 2006."

"1968?" I said. "Wasn't that when Charlotte Rawlings died?"

"It was," Walker confirmed. "Her death was officially ruled a boating accident, but Sullivan documented a suspicious fire at her apartment the night of the day she died. The apartment was gutted. Everything was destroyed, including any evidence she might have kept there."

"It fits the pattern," Kate said.

Dr. Walker nodded, his breath wheezing slightly with the effort of speaking. "The pattern remains consistent throughout," he said. "You eliminate the witness, destroy the evidence, and control the narrative."

I studied the security records more carefully, noticing a recurring name, William Harris.

"Who's this Harris guy?" I asked.

"Ah, now that's where it gets interesting," Sarah replied. "William Harris was Elizabeth's half-brother from her father's affair with a housekeeper. He was in charge of security at the Mason mill during the fire."

"Another family connection," Kate said.

"Harris wasn't just any security guard," Dr. Walker continued. "After the mill fire, he became the nominal head of security operations for both families, while publicly appearing to work only for the Rawlings."

The personnel files showed Harris's remarkable longevity - serving from the 1940s until his death in 1995, his position then passing to his son Robert.

"His descendants now work for both families," Sarah explained.

"There are financial transfers to William Harris dating back to 1947," Sarah continued. "Monthly payments from both families channeled to him through Swiss numbered accounts."

"The same accounts that handled the Nazi gold?" I asked.

"Yes. Exactly," Sarah replied. "Initially they were labeled as 'compensation for special services,' later, after he formally joined the Rawlings staff, they were documented as 'consulting fees.'"

The pattern was becoming clear. "So this guy Harris was compensated for his role in the mill fire, then elevated to oversee joint security operations."

"And there's more," Walker continued, nodding his head. "We found Harris's personal logs. He kept detailed records of every operation he oversaw, including Elizabeth's surveillance during the months before her death."

"That's direct evidence connecting the security operations to her murder," Sarah muttered.

I shook my head. "No, it's circumstantial. Just because they were watching her, it doesn't mean they had a hand in her death."

Walker nodded and continued, "As you say, Harry, but it's clear that Elizabeth's own half-brother helped maintain the system that eventually killed her," he said quietly.

"It also appears that the Harris family created their own power base," Sarah added, "using their knowledge of family secrets as leverage."

I nodded to Kate, who was already drafting requests for additional search warrants. "We need to locate Robert Harris," she said. "If he has his father's records..." she trailed off.

"He'll have the documentation of every operation both families conducted for decades," I finished for her. "Including Elizabeth's murder. Hmm, I wonder..."

I picked up my phone and called Eleanor Rawlings.

"Sergeant Starke," she said. "How nice. What can I do for you?"

"Good morning, Mrs. Rawlings," I said. "I'm hoping you can help me one more time."

"If I can," she replied.

"I'm going to put you on speaker," I said. "If that's alright with you."

"Of course," she replied.

"What do you know about Elizabeth's half-brother, William Harris?" I asked. "We've just discovered his role in the families' security operations," I told her.

"Have you, now?" she said. "More than I want to," she continued. "Harris wasn't just Elizabeth's half-brother. He was also Thomas Mason's illegitimate son's half-brother. Both from the same housekeeper."

At that, I blinked. The revelation landed like a physical blow. Not only that, I was struggling to get my head around it. "So the night watchman, one of the three who died in the fire…"

"…was also Harris's half-brother," she finished for me. She sounded somber as she continued, "Yes, Harris helped orchestrate the fire that killed his own brother."

"Why would he do that?" I asked.

"For the same reason anyone else in this cockeyed family did anything; power and money. William Harris was smart. He leveraged his knowledge of both families' secrets to create his own little dynasty within the families' structure."

After ending the call, I looked around the room. For several moments, nobody said anything as we processed the implications of what we'd just heard.

Finally, Walker shook his head and said, "I didn't think there was any more to learn, but…" he trailed off.

"Robert Harris's last known address is at a property owned by one of the Mason shell companies," Sarah said, looking up from her laptop. "We should move quickly before he destroys his father's records."

I shook my head. "If he was going to do that, he would have done it weeks ago," I said. "But we do need a warrant for that address. Kate, see to it, will you, please. Judge Strange should be in his chambers."

She nodded, jumped up, and almost ran from the room to return an hour later, warrant in hand.

In the meantime, I called Chief Johnston and arranged for

Mike Willis and his team to secure Harris's residence, but my instincts were telling me we were already too late. If Harris had been monitoring the investigation as his father would have, the evidence would have already have been destroyed.

While waiting for Kate to return with the warrant, Walker, Sarah, and I continued reviewing Sullivan's fire analysis. The retired fire marshal had documented distinctive patterns in each incident: accelerant points, spread methodology, timing. It seemed the families had developed a signature approach to evidence elimination.

"Recent fires follow the exact same pattern," Sarah noted, comparing Sullivan's documentation with preliminary reports from recent incidents. "They're still using the original playbook."

"Because it worked," I replied.

Dr. Walker's oxygen supply hissed softly as he leaned forward. "Elizabeth must have known," he said, thoughtfully, "which is why she distributed her own evidence so widely. She ensured no single fire could eliminate everything."

EMBERS OF 47
Monday, October 29, 11am

WE ARRIVED at the Harris's residence at just before eleven that morning to find it empty. I walked around the house to the back door. It, too, was locked. I stepped down off the deck into the backyard where, just beyond and to the right of the deck, I spotted the remains of a fire that had been started two days earlier. The next-door neighbor had called it in because it was unattended, and the fire department had extinguished it before the materials had been completely destroyed. Fortunately, Mike was able to recover a quantity of partially burned paperwork.

"What we have here," he said as I stood beside him, "appear to be security logs, surveillance reports. And..." he paused as he looked around, "It looks like Harris left in a hurry."

And with that and a disgusted shake of the head, I left him to it with instructions to get a breakdown of the damaged records to me ASAP.

"So, I was right," I muttered to myself as I joined Kate, and we walked together back to the car.

"Put out a BOLO for Harris," I said to Kate as I started the engine. "I've just about had enough of this mess. It's gone on far too long. We need to close it down now. And stay on Willis. I want what's in those recovered documents soonest."

"That's likely to take a while; you know that," she said.

"Yeah, well, just stay on him anyway," I muttered.

Twenty minutes later, I was sitting in front of the chief's desk, filling him in on this latest development. That done, I sat back in my chair and stared at him. The famous mustache was literally bristling as he worked his mouth from one side to the other. It would have been funny had the situation not been as serious as it was.

"We need to get this done, Sergeant," he snapped. "The federal prosecutor has enough for indictments on the RICO case, but if we can connect the historical crimes to current operations, so much the better."

"We're trying to establish that pattern now," I assured him. "Harris tried to burn his records, but I'm hoping there's enough left—"

"We need Robert Harris himself," Johnston snapped, cutting me off.

"And we're on that, too," I said. "We have a BOLO out for him, but he seems to have disappeared like... smoke," I finished, lamely.

The chief nodded grimly. "Just like his father would have taught him," he said. "These families have been disappearing evidence and witnesses for far too long. Get it done, Harry. You can go!"

And I did, but I was too frustrated to be able to do anything constructive, so I grabbed Kate, left the two Walkers in my office, going through the records for the umpteenth time, and we got out of there.

"Late lunch?" I said as I started the car.

She looked at her watch. "It's almost two-fifteen..." she trailed off when she saw the look I was giving her. "Sure," she said. "I guess it didn't go well, then, your meeting with the chief?"

"What do *you* think?" I replied savagely and then immediately regretted snapping at her. "Sorry, Kate... I didn't mean... No, it didn't. He's pissed, and he wants the case over and done with, and so do I, damn it."

We spent the next hour at the Boathouse restaurant on Riverfront Parkway, ostensibly talking about the case. But in fact, we did no such thing. We had a quiet, studiously quiet, lunch and, for the most part, we ate in silence, and when we did speak, it wasn't about the case.

"We'd better get back," Kate said, finally.

I looked at my watch and nodded.

It was almost three-thirty when we arrived back at my office.

"Your CSI supervisor came by a little while ago," Sarah said as we entered. "He said to tell you he'd had his team photograph all they could of the burned paperwork and that he put the images on a flash drive. It's on your desk. He also said to tell you he thinks you got lucky, whatever that means."

I sat down at my desk and inserted the flash drive into my desktop computer and began to flip through the images. As Willis said, and as we'd hoped, we had indeed gotten lucky. It's amazing how long it takes for thick wads of paper to burn. Some of the stuff was almost intact, though severely scorched.

William Harris had maintained meticulous records of his operations, and so had his son, Robert, including the surveillance of Elizabeth Rawlings during the months before her murder.

"Anything good?" Kate said, standing behind me, looking over my shoulder.

"Yeah, I think so," I replied. I made her a copy of the thumb drive and asked her to see what she could find among the literally hundreds of scraps of burned paper.

It was almost an hour later, at around four-thirty, when I came across the most damning evidence, a scorched record of the meeting where Elizabeth's "containment" was authorized. Notes in Robert Harris's precise handwriting documenting the patriarchs' decision that she had become a liability requiring a 'permanent solution.'

"This directly connects both Thomas Mason and James Rawlings Jr. to Elizabeth's murder," I said, printing out the crucial pages. "Conspiracy to commit murder charges with solid documentation. All we need is a handwriting comparison."

My phone rang. Robert Harris had been apprehended thirty miles away at the Cleveland Regional Jetport, attempting to board a private jet. The said jet was registered to a shell company connected to… you guessed it, the families.

"He had a briefcase full of documents," the Cleveland police sergeant said, "And electronic storage: hard drives and flash drives. You want us to deliver him, or d'you want to come and get him?"

"I'll send someone to get him," I replied. "And thank you, Sergeant."

I hung up and turned to Kate and said, "It looks like Robert was taking his insurance policy with him." I told them what the sergeant had told me. Then I picked up my desk phone and called for a car to go to Cleveland and pick up Harris.

"Smart move," Kate said after I hung up.

I looked at Dr. Walker. He looked worn out, fragile.

"You two need to go home," I said. "You've done enough. We can take it from here."

"Thank you for all you've done, Harry. You, too, Kate," he said. "Elizabeth would have been proud to know you, I'm sure."

"She died in my arms," I replied. "It doesn't get more personal than that."

"That is true, my friend," he said, and looked up at Sarah, the signal that he was ready to go.

"Will you testify before the grand jury?" I asked him.

"If they ask me to, and if my health permits," he replied. "I owe it to Elizabeth to see it through to the end."

And so do I, I thought as I watched the officer push the wheelchair across the situation room to the elevator. *And so do I!*

As evening approached, Kate and I finalized our report for the federal prosecutor. The evidence was overwhelming. We had financial records spanning three decades, security logs documenting criminal operations, and we had direct connections between historical crimes and current activities.

"Wow," Kate said. "I've never seen anything like it. Three generations of crimes all neatly tied together. From Nazi gold to international art theft."

"And the Harris family provided the final thread," I said. "The one we needed most, along with him, of course. Now we just need to get him to talk."

I called the prosecutor's office and told them we were on our way, and I was put through to the lady herself, Amy Stern, who said she'd wait for us.

It was a little after six-thirty when Kate and I arrived at the federal building and delivered our report. Stern's satisfaction was evident by the smile on her face as she reviewed our findings.

"This completes what Elizabeth Rawlings started," she said. "The grand jury will have everything they need to recommend a true bill on all charges. By the way, Caroline Mitchell will handle the proceedings."

It was almost nine o'clock when we left the federal building. The evening air carried the familiar scents of the river. Robert Harris was being processed at the federal detention center. His father's meticulous records, along with his own, were now key evidence against the families they'd served.

Me? I was in a somewhat pensive mood as Kate and I sat together on the covered patio at my home, glass in hand, thinking about the events of the past weeks. "Echoes of 1947," I said, looking out over the river. "Still reverberating through the present. What the hell were those old men thinking? They had everything a person could want."

"Wasn't it the English Lord Acton who stated, 'Power tends to corrupt and absolute power corrupts absolutely?'" Kate asked.

I smiled at her and said, "Geez, Kate, where did that come from?"

"I'm not just a pretty face, you know," she said loftily.

"I never said you were, far from it," I replied. "In fact," I chose my words carefully, "you're really quite beautiful."

She looked at me, frowning. "Quite?" she asked. "What *exactly* does that mean?"

"All right," I said. "You're very beautiful, exceedingly beautiful, exquisite, in fact. There, how does that suit you?"

She pursed her lips, frowned, then burst out laughing. Then she leaned in close, kissed me on the cheek, and said, "You *are* a fool sometimes, Harry Starke, but thank you. Quite was just perfect. Not too little, not too much."

And then she turned serious again. "Full circle," she said. "It started with the fire that started it all, continued through the pattern of fires that followed, and ended with the final fire in Robert Harris' back yard. It's kind of poetic, don't you think?"

"Not really," I replied, dryly.

"Awe, come on, Harry," she replied, and… "Well, you get the idea."

———

Frank Sullivan's memorial service was held at the old fire station where he'd begun his career. Kate and I attended, of course. The overall attendance was small, mostly retired firefighters and a few investigators who had worked with him over the years. His family had long since scattered, connections frayed by his decades-long obsession with the mill fire.

"He never stopped looking for the truth," one retired firefighter told us. "Even when everyone said he was chasing ghosts."

Ghosts? I thought. *I don't think so.* Frank Sullivan had finally been vindicated. His careful documentation of the fire patterns had proved crucial to establishing the families' methodology, and the web of lies had finally crumbled, exposed by a fire investigator who refused to accept the official narrative.

After the service, we drove to the hospital to check on Dr. Walker. Sarah met us in the hallway, her expression troubled.

"He's had a setback," she said. "His doctor's concerned about his oxygen levels."

"Is he going to be okay?" Kate asked.

"The doctor says he is, but he needs complete rest. No more case work for now."

I nodded. "He's done enough," I said. "We have everything we need for the prosecutors to make their case."

Sarah looked relieved. "I told him that, but he's determined to see this through personally. Elizabeth was his friend."

"Tell him we've submitted the final report," Kate said. "Just as Elizabeth would have wanted."

"I will," she said.

As we left the hospital, I received a text informing me the grand jury would convene in three days, with indictments expected on all charges: money laundering, art theft, tax evasion, and RICO violations.

"It's really happening," Kate said when I shared the news. "After all this time, they're finally facing justice."

It was dark by the time we reached my riverside condo and I was in a good mood, probably for the first time since the night Elizabeth Rawlings died in my arms.

"I think it's time for a little celebration," I said as I took a bottle of Moet from the refrigerator. I popped the cork, poured two tall glasses, and we went to the couch in front of the windows. The waters of the Tennessee were smooth as glass that night, but something was happening on the Thrasher bridge. A fire was blazing—a car—and the reflections of the red lights on the fire trucks were turning the Tennessee into a river of blood.

Kind of appropriate, I thought as I raised my glass and said, "To Frank Sullivan, may God bless him.

"To Frank," Kate muttered and took a sip of her Champagne.

The fire on the bridge was quickly subdued and the fire trucks left. A momentary breeze stirred the quiet waters and the reflected lights on the bridge turned them into scattered gold, a fitting reminder of the Nazi plunder that had started it all.

I thought of William Harris, orchestrating the fire that killed his own half-brother, then spending decades covering it up, and the twisted loyalty that had sustained the families' criminal enterprise.

I took a sip of Champagne, still deep in thought.

"A penny for your thoughts," Kate said, snuggling up to me.

"You know," I said, "It's never the same; the river. Every night it's different. Sometimes wild, sometimes so quiet it looks frozen. I love it out here."

"I know you do," she said. "And I don't blame you. It's... quite beautiful," she finished and smiled at me.

I smiled back at her, catching her drift. "Exquisite," I said.

We sat close together, my arm around her shoulders. "You know, Sullivan was right," I said after several moments. "It always comes back to blood, doesn't it? Family blood, I mean."

Outside, the river continued its eternal journey, carrying the echoes of the past toward an uncertain future. And somewhere in the city, construction equipment stood ready at the North Shore development site. Elizabeth's final project was proceeding under federal oversight. The foundations on Cameron Hill had already been laid, and construction of the new Blue Cross Blue Shield building was about to begin.

The echoes of 1947 would continue to resonate, but now as cautionary lessons rather than protected secrets. Elizabeth Rawlings had ensured that much, at least.

And then I had another thought. *Jack Marshall?*

BLOOD TRUST
   Thursday, November 1

THE GRAND JURY proceedings began exactly as the federal prosecutor had predicted and ended with indictments on all charges against both families' patriarchs and key members of their organizations. The evidence was simply too overwhelming to dispute, though that didn't stop their attorneys from trying.

I testified for nearly four hours, laying out the connections between Elizabeth's murder and the broader criminal enterprise. Kate followed with another two hours, focused on the financial aspects of the investigation. By day's end, there was little doubt about the outcome.

"You look exhausted," Kate said, as we left the federal building.

The November afternoon had turned cold, the sky overcast, gray clouds threatening rain.

"Four hours explaining three generations of crime will do that to you." I replied as I checked my phone. "Crap," I said, seeing three missed calls from Chief Johnston and a text from Sarah Walker reporting her father's condition had stabilized.

We'd barely reached my car when my phone rang again. It was Eleanor Rawlings.

"Harry," she said without preamble, "I've found something about the family trust you need to see immediately."

Oh geez, I thought. *Not more, surely?*

"What kind of something?" I asked.

"The kind that explains how they've been able to maintain control of downtown real estate despite appearing to fight over every piece of property," she said urgently. "This isn't just another shell company, Harry. It's the foundation of... well, everything."

I glanced at Kate, who nodded. "Text us the location," I said wearily. "We'll come now." I lookad at my watch. It was just after four-thirty. It looked like the long day was about to turn into an even longer night.

Eleanor had been moved to a safe house on Signal Mountain, a modest home with a sweeping view of the Tennessee River valley. Federal protection officers verified our identities before allowing us inside, where we found Eleanor surrounded by financial documents and property deeds.

"This is what they called the Blood Trust," she said, gesturing to the papers spread across a dining table. "That's what they called it internally. Seriously. I'm not kidding, Harry. It's the legal entity that actually controls most of downtown Chattanooga's historic properties."

I examined the documents, recognizing the complex legal structures establishing a trust in 1942, initially funded with proceeds from the gold smelting operation.

"This isn't in any of the records we've reviewed," Kate said as she photographed key pages with her Nikon Coolpix digital camera.

"That's because it was established under Swiss banking laws, then filtered through five shell companies before appearing in the American records." Eleanor replied. "The legal structure was designed to be impenetrable, even to federal investigators."

As I studied the trust documents, the scale became clear. It covered properties throughout downtown, riverfront developments, historic buildings, all controlled by an entity jointly owned by both families while publicly appearing to belong to one or the other.

Meanwhile, Kate was examining property maps highlighting trust-owned buildings. "These properties align with the tunnel system access points," she muttered.

"Of course they do," Eleanor said. "Almost all of them have basements that are now part of Chattanooga's Underground. The trust was specifically created to protect the families' smuggling infrastructure. The public disputes distracted attention from the true purpose, which was to maintain joint control of the properties that connected to the tunnel network."

My phone buzzed. It was Chief Johnston again. I stepped outside to take the call while Kate continued examining the trust documents.

"Where are you, Harry?" the chief demanded. "I've been trying to reach you since this afternoon."

"I've been testifying before the grand jury for four hours and now I'm at the Rawlings estate following up on new evidence about the Mason and Rawlings family trust," I explained. "Eleanor's found documentation of the legal entity controlling their joint assets."

"That's nice," he said, sarcastically, "but it's going to have to wait. We have a situation, and I need you here at the department. Lieutenant Marshall escaped federal custody an hour ago."

"What?" I closed my eyes. "You're kidding me," I snapped. "How the hell did that happen?"

"Medical transport," the chief replied. "Both officers are down, one critically wounded. Marshall took their weapons and vehicle."

"Geez! Any leads on his location?" I asked.

"He was last seen heading toward downtown. There's a BOLO out to all agencies." The chief paused, then, "Harry, he was heard saying something about a contingency plan."

"Contingency plan?" I asked, frowning.

"Apparently, the families set up some sort of emergency protocol for their key people," Johnston explained. "Escape routes, offshore accounts, new identities, and so on. Marshall knows he's facing life in prison. He's making a run for it."

"And he needs access to those resources," I said thoughtfully. "That's why he's heading downtown."

"That is the most likely reason," Johnston said. "We've put security on all the family properties we know about, but if what he needs is stored somewhere else..." the chief trailed off.

"He'll go to Plan B," I said. "He'll need a hostage... and the only person of interest in the downtown area is Dr. Walker." I said. "And he's at Siskin for rehab. That's where Marshall's headed."

"Then you'd better get over there," Johnston snapped. "If anything happens to Walker, there'll be hell to pay."

"I'm on it," I replied, but I was too late. He'd already hung up.

After the call, I returned to find Kate and Eleanor deep in discussion about the trust's financial structure.

"Sorry, ladies," I said. "This will have to wait. We need to move," I told them, and explained Marshall's escape. "I don't think he's coming here, but obviously he knows about this location." Eleanor looked alarmed.

"He does? How?" she asked.

"He's been the families' inside man for twenty years," I replied. "He's had access to everything. He knows what we know."

I stepped over to the window where I could see two federal agents walking the grounds, but I didn't trust that Marshall couldn't get past them if he decided Eleanor was his target. He knew the protection protocols inside and out.

"Is there somewhere else we can take these documents?" I

asked Eleanor. "There's no need," she replied. "Everything is digitized, and I've already sent copies to the federal prosecutor."

As we prepared to leave, my phone rang again. It was Sarah Walker, and she was obviously in distress.

"Harry," she said, her voice tight with fear, "someone's trying to get into Dad's hospital room and—"

I could hear a commotion in the background interrupting her, followed by what sounded like a struggle. The call ended abruptly.

"I knew it," I snapped. "Marshall's going after Walker," I said, but Kate was already moving toward the door. "Call for backup at the hospital while I get Eleanor somewhere secure."

"I'm coming with you," Kate insisted. "Eleanor has federal protection. They'll handle it."

The agents confirmed they'd move Eleanor to a different location immediately, and we left them to it.

As we rushed to my car, I called the chief to alert him about the situation at the hospital, but he already knew. "SWAT's already en route," he said, "but, Harry, be careful. Marshall's smart, and he knows how we operate. He'll be anticipating our response."

He didn't have to tell me that. I already knew how smart he was. He had to be to operate within the system for so long and not get outed.

The drive to the hospital took an agonizing fifteen minutes, even with lights and siren. When we arrived, we found a scene of controlled chaos. Hospital security had implemented their own lockdown procedures. Police units—PD's and sheriff's—surrounded the building, and SWAT was preparing to enter. By then it was after six-thirty.

"Geez, what a mess," I said to Kate as I pulled to a stop among the assembled units near the SWAT vehicle.

"What's the situation?" I asked the SWAT commander. His tag identified him as Lieutenant Marc Simmons.

"As far as we can tell, we have a single suspect barricaded in a room on the third floor of the east wing. He has four hostages. Dr. Walker, his daughter, a nurse, and one of your officers."

"Lieutenant Marshall?" I asked, already knowing the answer.

Simmons nodded. "Yup, we have him on the hospital security system. The cameras recorded him from entry to the room. He doesn't seem to give a damn. He has made contact, though. He's demanding safe passage out of the building and access to a safe deposit box."

I thought quickly. "Let me talk to him. I know what he really wants."

"Negative, Sergeant," Simmon's said. "SWAT has operational control and we're about to—"

My phone buzzed—an unknown number. I held up my hand, cutting him off and answered the call.

"Hello, Harry," Marshall said, his voice unnervingly calm. "I figured you'd show up, eventually. You going to give me what I want, or do I have to start killing my hostages?"

"Let them go, Jack," I said. "You know I don't have the authority to negotiate. You're already in enough trouble. You want to add first degree homicide to the list?"

"I already have what I need," he replied. "The academic knows what I want and where it is." Marshall's voice was tense despite his efforts to maintain control. "I want the account numbers and the contact information for the family identity specialists. What I want from *you* is safe passage out of here."

"You're not getting out of this, Jack," I said. "The Masons and the Rawlings are locked up; they're done. There's nowhere you can run, nowhere you can hide the feds won't find you."

"Oh yeah?" he snapped. "How about the twenty years of secrets I have that they don't want exposed? That's enough leverage for me to disappear. So, do I get safe passage or not?"

I glanced at Simmons, who was monitoring the call. He nodded.

"What exactly is it you want, Jack?" I asked.

"I want access to the family safe deposit box at First Tennessee Bank. That's where they keep what I need. I have the key and the box number. I just need to get to it… and a way out of here."

I looked again at the SWAT commander. He shook his head.

"You know I can't do that, Jack. One, I don't have the rank and two," I looked at the commander, then continued, "the SWAT commander is itching to get in there."

"That happens, Harry, and all you'll get is five dead bodies. Now talk to the chief and tell him what I want. Don't play games with me, Harry. I need access to that box, and I need it now. You do what I say and everyone walks away happy."

Simmons was already coordinating with his team, using Marshall's call to pinpoint his exact location.

"Look, Jack. Why don't you let me come up there?" I said, desperately looking for a way to stop the situation from escalating out of hand. "We can work it out face to face."

"You think I'm stupid, Starke?" he asked. "You just want to buy some time so SWAT can come bustin' in here. I don't think so." Marshall laughed humorlessly. "Here's what's going to happen. You're going to clear a path to the parking garage. Once I'm in a vehicle with Walker and the girl, you'll arrange the bank access."

"That's not happening, Jack."

"Then the professor's daughter dies first." His voice was hard, cold, and I had no doubt he meant it.

"You have ten minutes to clear that path, Starke. Now get to it."

After he hung up, I turned to Simmons and said, "He's desperate. He needs what's in a safe deposit box. It's at First Tennessee at Hamilton Place. It contains escape protocols, account numbers, contacts for new identities, and safe houses."

"We have snipers in position," Simmons replied, "but no clear shot. He's using the hostages as shields."

Kate, who'd been conferring with other officers, gathering information, joined us. She'd heard what I said.

"Marshall knows it's his only chance to escape federal prosecution," she said. "He won't go down easily."

"This could get nasty in a hurry," Simmons muttered, his hand to his earpiece, looking up at the third-floor windows. "He has the hostages at the windows. He's using them as shields."

"He knows our protocols," I said. "Twenty years in the department taught him exactly how we'd respond."

"So what do we do?" Kate asked.

My phone rang again. "Time's running out, Harry," Marshall said. "You gonna do what I say, or do I start killing people?"

"You know the drill, Jack. I need to know they're alive and unharmed," I said.

"Of course you do," he replied. There was a brief pause, then Sarah Walker's voice, shaky but clear, said, "Harry, he has a gun to my father's head. Please do what he asks."

And then, in the background, I heard Dr. Walker speak, weaker but determined, "Sergeant, do not give him access to those accounts—"

He was cut off as Marshall took back the phone. "Satisfied?" he asked. "Now clear that path, damn it."

"I need time to coordinate," I stalled. "The hospital's surrounded. I can't just wave everyone away. You know that."

"Ten minutes," Marshall said, then repeated, "Ten minutes and then I start shooting hostages." And he ended the call without waiting for an answer.

I looked at the tactical commander, lost for ideas. I knew we couldn't do what Marshall asked, but neither could we let him kill the hostages.

"We've accessed the hospital's ventilation system," Simmons said. "We might be able to introduce a sedative gas to incapacitate him before he can harm the hostages. What d'you think?"

"It's too risky," I said, shaking my head. "Dr. Walker has serious respiratory issues. The gas could kill him."

"Then we're out of options, Sergeant."

My mind raced, considering angles Marshall might not have anticipated.

"What if we give him what he actually wants - a way out?" I suggested, thinking aloud.

"What do you mean?" Simmons asked, frowning.

"Look, Marshall knows he's finished," I said. "He's desperate. He just wants to escape, and he thinks Walker has information that can help him do that." I turned to Kate. "We offer him a vehicle. Keys in the ignition, and a clear path out of the garage. Simple and believable."

"He'll never buy that," Simmons objected. "I sure as hell wouldn't."

"He might if he thinks it's his only option, and it's exactly what he's asking for," Kate said, catching on. "Right now, he's cornered. Give him what looks like an escape route, and he'll take it, giving us a chance to take him down."

"That wasn't quite what I was thinking," I said. "But the safety of the hostages is paramount. We need to get them away from him."

When Marshall called again, I made the offer. "Jack, here's the deal. We give you a vehicle, clear path out of the garage, and you have thirty minutes before we put out an APB. You take the officer with you and let him go when you're clear. You let the rest of the hostages go, and you get to walk away."

He was silent for a moment, then said, "And I'm supposed to believe that?" he scoffed.

"What choice do you have?" I asked. "You're surrounded. This is your only shot at getting out of here alive."

"I need money, Harry, and documents," he replied.

"No money, no documents. You have my offer," I said. "What's it to be?"

The silence as he considered the option was palpable. "You bring the keys yourself," he said, finally. "And you come alone."

Simmons was already shaking his head, but I nodded. "Deal," I snapped. "Five minutes."

After ending the call, Simmons confronted me. "Are you out of your mind? This is not happening, Sergeant."

"It's our best option," I argued. "Marshall's desperate, not stupid. He knows a hostage standoff only ends one way, with him dead. But if he thinks he has a chance to escape..." I trailed off.

"And when he realizes it's a trap?" Simmons countered.

"By then, we'll have the hostages," I said, grinning at him.

Reluctantly, Simmons nodded and, within minutes, I was wearing a thin body armor vest under my jacket and had a set of car keys in my hand.

"This is insane," Kate muttered as she helped adjust the vest.

"Trust me. It'll work," I replied, though my confidence was mostly for show. "He knows it's the only chance he's got."

The hospital corridor was eerily silent as I approached Walker's room. SWAT team members had secured positions at the corridor junctions, out of sight but ready to move.

"I'm here, Jack," I called out, stopping several feet from the door. "Just me, with the keys."

The door opened a crack. "Show me your hands," Marshall shouted. "Turn around slowly."

I complied, jangling the keys to show that's all I carried. "Let the hostages go, and you can walk out of here."

After a moment, the door opened slowly to reveal Marshall slowly backing away, his weapon trained on me. "Come on in. Slow and easy."

I entered carefully, my movements slow and deliberate as he said. The room was a mess. Dr. Walker was in his wheelchair, his oxygen tank beside him, while Sarah knelt on the floor nearby. The security guard was sitting, leaning against the wall, a nasty looking wound to his temple. The nurse, a pretty young woman, was seated beside him, her face as white as the proverbial sheet.

"You okay?" I asked.

She nodded, but didn't reply.

Marshall stood to one side, his weapon in his right hand trained steadily on Walker, his other hand extended toward me, palm up. "The keys," he demanded.

"First, I need to see the hostages are unharmed," I insisted, making eye contact with Sarah.

"They're fine," Marshall snapped. "Gimme the frickin' keys, Starke. Now."

I held them up. "Blue Chevy truck in the south garage, level two, parked next to the elevator, just to the right as you exit. The barrier's open. All you have to do is drive out without stopping and you're free and clear, but I get the hostages first."

Marshall studied me, suspicion clear in his narrowed eyes. "Something's not right," he said. "Why would you help me escape?"

I shrugged. "It's all about the hostages, Jack. I'd rather chase you tomorrow than attend four funerals."

Something in my tone must have convinced him. He gestured toward the door with his gun. "The girl goes first, then the nurse... No, she goes with me. The guard goes next, then the old man."

"The deal was—"

"I know what the deal was," he snarled. "I'm changing it. The girl goes with me. I'll let her go when I'm..." he thought for a moment, then said, "when I'm clear."

Sarah looked at me questioningly. I nodded, and she slowly rose to her feet.

"Go," Marshall ordered. "No tricks."

As Sarah moved toward the door, I stayed perfectly still, watching Marshall's trigger finger. The guard followed, then

Walker, obviously struggling to propel the chair. I would have helped him, but I had to keep an eye on Marshall.

Once they were clear, Marshall gestured with his weapon. "The keys," he said. "Slide them across the floor."

I obeyed, and he snatched them up without taking his eyes or his gun off me and the nurse.

"Now, Starke, back up against the wall."

I complied, positioning myself where the SWAT team could see me through the window, and Marshall began backing toward the door, keeping his weapon trained on us.

"If anyone follows me before I reach the car, the girl dies," he snarled.

"You have thirty minutes," I said.

He reached the door, the gun still aimed at me. "One more thing, Starke. This isn't over between us. You'll see."

Just as he started to turn, something happened out in the corridor. Dr. Walker, the effort of propelling the wheelchair too much for him, slumped in his chair, his oxygen monitor alarm blaring. Marshall's attention wavered for just a split second—and that was all the SWAT team needed.

They burst in through the door and windows simultaneously as I dived at Marshall. He managed to get one shot off as I hit him and rolled. The shot went wide and before he could fire again, he was tackled to the ground by three SWAT officers.

It was over in seconds.

The medical team rushed in to check on Walker, whose perceived "collapse" had been perfectly timed. "Nicely done, Sergeant," one of the SWAT officers said as he helped me to my feet.

"Not me," I replied, looking at Walker, who was now sitting upright again, a sly smile on his face despite his genuine respiratory distress.

Marshall, now in cuffs, collapsed against the wall as I picked up his weapon and handed it to the officer.

The medical response was immediate, a hospital trauma team rushing along the corridor to assess Marshall while other personnel attended to the hostages. Dr. Walker's oxygen levels had dropped dangerously low during the incident and required immediate intervention. The nurse, whose name I learned later was Charlie, was unharmed. Sarah, too, was unharmed but clearly in shock. The hostage officer had a concussion from a blow from the gun but was otherwise stable.

"Your timing was perfect," I told Simmons as the situation stabilized.

"Your distraction gave us the window we needed," he acknowledged. "Though, I still think you took an unnecessary risk."

Perhaps he was right, but the outcome justified the means, as they say. Marshall was taken away, his hands shackled behind his back, muttering obscenities, most of them aimed at me.

It was a good result. The hostages were safe, and a desperate man's final attempt to escape justice had been thwarted. Hours later, after statements had been taken, and the scene processed, Kate and I sat in the hospital cafeteria, the adrenaline crash having left us exhausted.

"Marshall was willing to kill to save himself," Kate said, staring into her coffee.

"The ultimate irony," I replied, "is that the man who protected the families' criminal enterprise was finally undone by the system he helped maintain. Kinda cool, don't you think?"

THE COVENANT
Friday, November 2, 10am

THE FOLLOWING MORNING, after a restful night, Kate and I joined the federal agents as they swarmed the oldest section of the Volunteer Valley Country Club, following coded coordinates lifted from Elizabeth Rawling's development plans. After a search of the wine cellar, they located the original meeting place where the two patriarchs had signed their covenant in 1947.

Kate and I arrived just as they breached the locked door to a room hidden behind a wheeled wine rack at the rear of the cellar and disguised as part of the brick wall during renovations in the 1960s. It could be opened with a key, but as they didn't have one, the feds did what they do best; they took a sledgehammer to it.

"Too bad they didn't wait for you," I muttered to Kate as I surveyed the damage.

The space was remarkably well preserved, a time capsule untouched for decades.

"Oh my," Kate said as she joined me at the entrance. "It's like walking back in time to 1947."

The room was twenty feet wide by thirty long. It was furnished with an oak conference table surrounded by ten leather chairs. Crystal decanters stood on a sideboard. Photographs on the wood-paneled walls showed both families together at various events, moments of collaboration carefully hidden from public view.

"So this is what Thomas Mason was doing the night Elizabeth was murdered," I said.

"This is where it all began," the federal CSI tech explained. "This is where they formalized their arrangement after the mill fire."

At the head of the table was a leather-bound portfolio, the covenant itself preserved under glass. And we watched as the techs carefully prepared the documented exhibit for removal and examination.

"The original agreement," the tech continued, "signed by both patriarchs on September 30, 1947, two weeks after the mill fire."

"Can we look?" I asked.

The tech nodded and handed us both a pair of white cotton gloves. "Ten minutes. Be careful," he said as he removed the glass cover and gently lifted the book out of the display case and placed it on the table.

The document was remarkable in its candor, detailing how both families would maintain public animosity while privately collaborating on joint enterprises, though there was no mention of criminality per se. It outlined profit-sharing arrangements, security protocols, and the establishment of the blood trust to hold shared assets.

Most damning was the explicit acknowledgment of their Nazi collaboration: *Whereas both parties have successfully cooperated in the acquisition and processing of European financial assets during the* recent conflict, and whereas such cooperation has proven mutually beneficial... etc., etc.

"European financial assets," Kate remarked. "Their terminology for Nazi gold."

"They weren't concerned about this document being discovered," I noted. "It was meant for family eyes only."

The covenant continued with procedures for maintaining their feud: scheduled public disputes, carefully choreographed legal battles, even guidelines for appropriate levels of apparent hostility in social settings.

"It's a complete playbook," the tech said as Kate photographed each page.

"Does it mention the Harris family?" I asked, remembering Dr. Walker's revelation about the true power structure.

"Yes, there's a section titled 'Security and Implementation,'" he replied. "It designates William Harris as Chief Security Officer for both families, with authority to enforce covenant terms and resolve disputes."

"Not just an employee, then," Kate observed.

The most revealing section detailed the blood trust's establishment and structure, confirmation of everything Eleanor Rawlings had discovered. The trust would hold certain downtown properties using Swiss banking laws and shell companies to obscure joint ownership. *Properties connected to the Underground*, I thought.

"The covenant is in-depth and wide-ranging," the technician said as he carefully turned the pages. "It's a complete framework for their enterprise, designed to last for generations."

As agents continued processing the room, they discovered recording devices hidden in light fixtures, modern surveillance equipment disguised as vintage elements.

"It's high-end equipment." Kate said, as she examined the surveillance setup. "They've obviously been recording their meetings, but where are they? The recordings?"

We found them stored on servers in an adjacent room, a comprehensive archive of family discussions spanning the last several years, the most recent dated just days before Elizabeth's murder, documenting the patriarchs discussing her investigation, the threat it posed, and the 'permanent solution,' as Thomas Mason put it.

"We have them on tape ordering the hit," Kate said, her voice tight with contained triumph. "Direct evidence of conspiracy to commit murder."

"The wording is a little ambiguous," I said, "perhaps even circumstantial. It could mean anything from paying her off to murder."

The federal prosecutor, Amy Stern, a woman of stature, aged forty-six ,with a no-nonsense reputation, arrived as technicians began transferring the recordings to evidence boxes. Her satisfaction was obvious by the thin smile as she surveyed the hidden meeting room.

"Elizabeth and Eleanor Rawlings built an extraordinary case, don't you think?" she said. "A little poetic justice, wouldn't you say, her being murdered to protect secrets hidden in the building where she died?"

I nodded. She was right, though I hadn't thought of it like that myself.

"This isn't just an agreement," Stern continued thoughtfully as she carefully turned the pages. "It's a binding document these two families regarded as sacred. Their honor was tied to upholding it, regardless of any moral implications."

"Family honor above all," I agreed.

"Precisely. The covenant *is* their moral framework, super-seding conventional ethics or legal constraints."

This psychological insight explained much about the families' behavior, their unwavering commitment to maintaining their system even when it required eliminating threats, even family members like Elizabeth or Charlotte.

The bounty the technicians recovered seemed never-ending: hundreds of damning documents, including the original banking records from the Nazi gold transfers.

"They kept everything," Kate muttered. "It's almost as if they were trying to bring about their own downfall. This stuff goes all the way back to 1938."

But the most damning evidence came from the surveillance archives, the recordings of family meetings where they openly discussed ongoing criminal operations, all carefully preserved as part of their meticulous record-keeping.

"Crazy," I muttered.

"Not really," the tech replied. "They just never expected anyone to penetrate this deep into their security. This room was their inner sanctum, protected by multiple layers of security."

As the afternoon approached, Eleanor Rawlings arrived at her own request—under federal protection—to examine the covenant. She was curious, of course, but it was her expertise and knowledge of the family history that made her particularly valuable in identifying individuals in the historical photographs and contextualizing documents.

"Elizabeth always suspected this room existed," she told me as she surveyed the room.

"How was that?" Kate asked.

"She found references to it in family correspondence, but it took her months to locate it."

"And how did she finally find it?" I asked.

"Through Thomas Mason's letters to Charlotte," Eleanor replied. "He mentioned meeting her here. 'Our secret place,' he called it, 'beneath the club where no one would think to look for us.'"

"So it was those love letters that provided the clue that uncovered three generations of criminal conspiracy," Kate said pensively. "Another irony in a case chock-full of them. It's... astonishing when you think about it."

Eleanor spent the next hour identifying individuals in the photographs lining the walls: family members, security personnel, and business associates spanning decades. Her encyclopedic knowledge of the families' connections proved invaluable as federal agents under the auspices of Amy Stern constructed relationship charts and family trees.

"This man," Eleanor said, pointing to a figure standing behind both patriarchs in a 1947 photograph, "is William Harris. He was the brains behind the covenant. He designed it to protect not only the two families, but first and foremost himself."

The photograph showed Harris in a subordinate position, but Eleanor's identification confirmed Dr. Walker's assessment of his actual authority. The servant strategically positioned to control the masters.

"It sounds like it was a true bureaucracy," I muttered.

"In its purest form," Eleanor agreed, and then continued, "The families maintained their feud in public while Harris engineered and implemented most of their joint operations from behind the scenes, and his descendants continued in the role right up until... now."

I shook my head, then turned to Stern and said, "I'd like to get a statement from Lieutenant Marshall. It's... an internal thing. He is one of ours."

"I'll arrange it," she replied, and took out her phone and made the call.

"Two o'clock this afternoon at the federal building," she said, "though I don't think you'll find him cooperative, but take all the time you need."

I turned to Kate and said, "I've had enough of this. You want to go get some lunch?"

"What d'you have in mind?" she asked, then added, "Not the country club. I'm not in the mood."

"Public House?" I asked.

She made a face. "Too busy."

"Where, then?" I asked.

"I fancy some good Chinese," she said. "How about PF Chang's?"

"Sounds good to me," I replied.

We said our goodbyes to Eleanor and Amy Stern, and we left them talking together.

Me? For once in the last few weeks, I felt at ease. No weird gut feelings.

Ruminations
Friday, November 2, 2pm

LUNCH WAS, as it always is at PF Chang's, excellent, and we left with my feeling of well being still intact. From there we headed downtown to the federal building, which is in itself a historic structure, being the location of the trial of Jimmy Hoffa back in 1964. Hoffa, president of the International Brotherhood of Teamsters, was tried and convicted for jury tampering and sentenced to eight years in federal prison. It was the beginning of the end for one of the most powerful men in the country.

We were conducted to an interview room where I found Marshall waiting for me, under guard and handcuffed to the table.

"Come to gloat, Starke?" he asked as we entered. "I see you brought your partner."

"We're here to get your statement for the record, Jack," I replied, setting up my recorder. "The federal prosecutor didn't think you'd want to talk to me," I said, using a little reverse psychology.

Marshall laughed humorlessly. "I'm sure she didn't. Well, she was wrong. I've got nothing to lose now. Might as well set the record straight." He locked eyes with me. "Maybe you'll put in a good word for me," he said, a sly look on his face.

"Maybe I will," I replied, "depending, of course, on how truthful you are."

Surprisingly, he was remarkably forthcoming. He detailed his recruitment by Robert Harris in 1999, his appointment to assist with 'family security matters,' and his gradual integration into the trust structure.

"Harris ran everything," Marshall said, confirming what we'd already learned. "Mason and Rawlings were the public faces, but Harris made the operational decisions. It's been that way since 1947."

"Including ordering Elizabeth's murder?" I asked

Marshall nodded. "Harris authorized it with approval from both patriarchs. Standard protocol for threats that couldn't be contained through normal channels."

"And your role in the operation?" Kate asked.

"Ensuring the investigation stayed contained. Redirecting department resources, monitoring your progress, reporting back to Harris." Marshall's admission was matter-of-fact. "With my years on the force, I knew exactly how to manage an investigation."

"Until Elizabeth's evidence started emerging," I said.

"She was smarter than anyone anticipated," Marshall acknowledged. "She distributed evidence, dead man's switches, federal contacts we didn't know about. By the time we realized what she'd done, it was too late; she had to go, a permanent solution, as Harris called it."

While we already knew most of his testimony, it added another layer to our understanding—confirmation from inside the operation of how the power structure actually functioned and how they responded to threats.

"One more question," I said as I prepared to leave. "Why did you target Dr. Walker specifically? What made him so dangerous?"

"He'd identified the Harris connection," Marshall replied without hesitation. "Most of the investigation was focused on Mason and Rawlings, but Walker was the only one who understood Harris was the power behind the thrones. That made him uniquely dangerous."

As evening approached, I dropped Kate off at her apartment, then returned to the covenant room for a final review before the transfer of the evidence. The federal team had completed their documentation and preserved the scene.

Amy Stern was just about to leave when I arrived.

"You're all done, then?" I asked.

"I think so," she replied. "The recordings alone are enough to convict them all."

"What about Elizabeth's murder?" I asked.

She made a face and shrugged. "I don't think we'll ever tie that down to a single individual. We know she was murdered, and we know they were all complicit, so conspiracy to commit murder will have to do."

We stood together at the doorway, staring pensively into the room. I don't know what Amy was thinking, but I was picturing the scene of the assembled families and their minions seated at the table, the air thick with cigar smoke, and I reflected on the significance of what we'd found.

"They never expected exposure," Amy said, reading my thoughts. "Three generations of infallible security made them complacent."

The last item to be removed from the covenant room was the glass-topped wooden case containing the leather portfolio that contained the original agreement.

"This is where it all began," I muttered.

"And where it ends," Amy added.

I took a last look at the empty room, now stripped of its furnishings, framed photographs and documents. It was a shell, but still somehow bearing witness to decades of secret meetings where two of Chattanooga's most powerful families had coordinated their criminal activities.

The covenant that had bound them was now evidence against them. The meeting place they'd protected for generations was exposed. The surveillance they'd maintained for their own records had, in fact, captured the very conversations that would prove their guilt.

Family honor had demanded loyalty to the covenant above all else. That same covenant, preserved with such care, would now destroy the empire built upon it.

"Two families bound by blood money and mutually assured destruction," Amy muttered.

It was during the afternoon on Monday, three days later that my phone rang. Amy Stern was calling to tell me that the grand jury had returned a true bill, indictments on all charges against both family patriarchs, Robert Harris, and the key members of their organizations. The charges included conspiracy to commit murder, money laundering, art theft, tax evasion, wire fraud and RICO violations.

"The covenant provided the connections we needed," she explained. "The recordings provided direct evidence of the original agreement and their guilt. We have them, Harry. Now we go to trial and put 'em away."

I ended the call, updated Kate, and then slipped out of the

office and made my way down to the first floor and to Chief Johnston's office.

Cindy looked up as I entered the outer office and looked quizzically at me.

"I need a few minutes," I said.

She nodded and picked up her phone. "Sergeant Starke is here to see you," she said, then listened, nodded, and hung up.

"You can go in," she said.

"Sit down, Harry," he said as I entered. He leaned back in his chair. "What d'you need? If you're here to tell me about the grand jury indictments, you're too late. Amy Stern called me ten minutes ago."

"Well, that was a waste of time," I said, beginning to stand up again.

"Sit down," he said. "I, too, have news. A federal asset forfeiture team has already begun seizure of the trust properties. Half of downtown Chattanooga is changing hands as we speak."

"No sh... I mean, wow," I corrected myself. "The families, what's left of them, must be imploding."

"Indeed," Johnston said. "The internal warfare has already started. The younger members, namely James Rawlings III and Margaret Mason, are trying to distance themselves from the patriarchs, claiming ignorance of the criminal enterprises."

"Seriously?" I asked, remembering the dealings I'd had with James. "James III is one sneaky... He's a liar and he can't be trusted. He was raised within the system, just like all the others. Indoctrinated from childhood to maintain the covenant at all costs. Chief, he used me—"

"Get over it, Harry," he said, nodding grimly. "Amy Stern and her team are evaluating offers of cooperation from various family members, including those two. Some of them appear genuinely ignorant of what was going on around them, while others—including young Rawlings and Mason—clearly participated knowingly, though there's no way to prove it. They either didn't attend the meetings or they kept their mouths shut."

"So they're not being charged with anything?" I asked, feeling cheated.

"At this moment, no," he replied. "But that doesn't mean they won't be."

"And the Harris family?" I asked. "What about them?"

"Robert Harris is cooperating fully in exchange for limited immunity," Johnston replied. "He's agreed to testify, and he's providing documentation that reaches into some highly placed political offices, regulatory agencies, and law enforcement across multiple jurisdictions. My prediction is he'll do a little time and then be ushered quietly into the federal witness protection program."

I shook my head. The implications were staggering. A criminal network extending far beyond Chattanooga, influencing officials and agencies throughout the Southeast.

But the good thing was—if anything about this mess was good—the family honor that had demanded absolute loyalty to the covenant for three generations was the same covenant that was about to bring them down. *How ironic,* I thought, *but justice for Elizabeth and all who had died protecting the family secrets.*

ATONEMENT

THE NEXT SEVERAL months went by quickly in a flurry of legal hearings, motions, and appeals, but it wasn't until May that things really began to speed up.

I remember that day well. The federal courthouse towered above Georgia Avenue, its limestone façade gleaming in the morning sunlight. A crowd had gathered outside: reporters, curious citizens, and representatives from both families attempting to distance themselves from the growing scandal. It was the day that marked the beginning of preliminary hearings for what the media had dubbed 'The Covenant Case.'

I parked in the multi-story on West 10th and walked across Miller Park, hoping to avoid the press gauntlet. Then I waited while Kate spent a few minutes with the federal attorney. This would be the first public airing of the full case against the Mason and Rawlings patriarchs, Robert Harris, and key members of their organizations. It was the day the judge would decide whether or not there was enough evidence to send them to trial.

"Quite the circus, huh?" I remarked as I joined Kate out front and together we passed through security to the elevator to the third floor, where the courtroom was situated.

"And getting bigger," Kate replied, nodding toward a group of well-dressed people. "Those are representatives from the World Jewish Congress and the WJRO, the World Jewish Restitution Organization. The looted art angle has garnered a lot of international attention."

The main third-floor corridor hummed with activity: federal agents conferring in hushed tones, attorneys reviewing documents, and family representatives maintaining a careful distance from each other.

The courtroom was already packed when we entered. Federal prosecutors had arranged an impressive display of evidence, the covenant portfolio on a central table, surrounded by financial records, art provenance documentation, and surveillance recordings.

"Wow!" Kate said. "No shortcuts here."

I nodded. "This is it," I said, gazing around the mahogany-paneled walls. "This was the beginning of the end for Jimmy Hoffa and, perhaps, for the Covenant families."

It wasn't the first time I'd been inside the historic courtroom, not by a long shot, but somehow this time it was different.

The prosecution strategy made sense: establish the covenant as the foundation for three generations of criminal activity, then demonstrate its continuity through documented operations to the present day. Simple, right? I surely hoped so.

Judge Marilyn Holcomb entered through a concealed door behind the bench. Her reputation for handling complex federal cases was well known. The courtroom fell silent as she surveyed the proceedings.

"Good morning, everyone," she began. "I'll say a few words and then we'll get to it. The goal of this preliminary hearing is to establish whether or not there is sufficient probable cause for the charges filed against the defendants, and for them to be bound over for trial. Given the scope and complexity of this case, the court anticipates a long and arduous procedure, during which I will brook no theatrics or histrionics."

The defendants sat in a row with their attorneys—Thomas Mason and James Rawlings Jr. looking undiminished in their tailored suits. Robert Harris maintained a professional composure, his military bearing evident even in custody. Their expressions ranged from defiance to resignation.

"Will you be making an opening statement, Ms. Mitchell?" the judge asked.

"Yes, your honor," Michell replied.

Holcomb nodded and said, "Please proceed and let's keep it short. This is a preliminary hearing, not a trial."

U.S. Attorney Caroline Mitchell stood and went to the lectern and began her presentation. It was methodical and comprehensive. She established the timeline from Nazi collaboration in the late 1930s through the mill fire of 1947, the covenant signing, and the subsequent decades of criminal enterprises.

"Your Honor, the United States will show that these defendants established and maintained a criminal enterprise spanning three generations," she explained. "This organization, formalized in a covenant signed in 1947, engaged in money laundering, tax evasion, art theft, wire fraud and ultimately conspiracy to commit murder when their operations were threatened with exposure."

The defense attorneys, led by Hector Carpenter, a naturalized Englishman, shifted uncomfortably in their seats as Mitchell outlined the evidence, particularly the surveillance recordings from the covenant room that captured the patriarchs discussing Elizabeth's 'containment.'

"The defendants were kind enough to document their criminal activities with remarkable thoroughness," Mitchell continued. "Their record-keeping provides irrefutable evidence of their ongoing operations from 1947 to the present day, including the conspiracy to murder Elizabeth Rawlings when she threatened to expose them."

And so it went on and on until, finally, she sat down and Hector Carpenter rose to make his opening statement. The man had a fascinating accent, but there was little he could say. He sat down again after only five minutes and the hearing got under way.

I was scheduled to testify second, after the federal agent who had led the covenant room evidence collection. Kate would follow me and Dr. Walker was scheduled to appear later in the proceedings, his testimony limited by his medical condition but considered essential for establishing context.

When called to the stand, I provided a comprehensive account of the investigation, from Elizabeth's murder through the discovery of the covenant room and the Harris family's role in the criminal enterprise. The defense attorneys attempted to challenge specific procedures, but the evidence was simply too overwhelming for procedural objections to gain traction.

"Detective Starke, in your professional assessment, what was the primary motivation for Elizabeth Rawlings' murder?" Mitchell asked as my testimony neared its conclusion.

"It's quite simple," I replied. "She was about to expose them, so they classified her as an 'existential threat' according to their covenant protocols, and authorized what they called a permanent solution. That permanent solution was, in fact, her elimination."

"And the Harris family's role in this decision?"

"Robert Harris was the families' third-generation security chief. He was responsible for the implementation of the permanent solution, as authorized by both patriarchs. He assigned the security team that carried out her murder, then coordinated with Lieutenant Marshall to ensure the investigation remained contained."

The defense objected to my characterization, but Judge

Holcomb overruled after Mitchell produced the specific covenant amendment, authorizing 'containment measures' for existential threats.

Kate's testimony followed. She established the financial connections between the Nazi gold, the blood trust, and the current criminal operations, including a PowerPoint presentation showing how the stolen assets were converted into cash and how it was then laundered into respectable family wealth.

"The blood trust wasn't just a legal entity holding real properties," she explained, highlighting key documents. "It was the financial infrastructure that connected historical crimes to present-day operations, allowing the families to maintain control of its assets."

During a brief recess, I spoke with Dr. Walker, who, despite his medical condition, insisted on giving evidence.

"The court needs to understand the historical context," he insisted. "They need to understand how the covenant created an alternate moral framework that justified their criminal activities."

"And your testimony will establish that foundation," I assured him. "The prosecutors have structured their case around the covenant as the organizing principle for everything that followed."

Walker nodded his approval.

When the proceedings resumed, a federal art crimes specialist testified about the recovered artifacts. She provided detailed provenance documentation connecting more than a dozen pieces of looted art to Jewish families who had lost everything during the Holocaust.

"The looted art isn't just valuable property," the specialist explained. "It represents cultural heritage stolen during humanity's darkest hour, then laundered through sophisticated channels established by the defendants."

As the day progressed, a remarkable pattern emerged in the defendants' reactions. The Mason and Rawlings patriarchs maintained aristocratic composure, their expressions suggesting this was merely an unfortunate business setback rather than the collapse of their criminal empire, while Robert Harris watched the proceedings, most of the time with his arms folded and his eyes narrowed. I assumed from his demeanor he was calculating the odds that his plea deal would be approved or not.

During the afternoon session, Eleanor Rawlings provided powerful testimony about the families' internal operations, the careful maintenance of their theatrical feud while actually collaborating. Her insider perspective proved devastating to the defense's attempts to minimize the coordination between the families.

"The public rivalry was meticulously choreographed," she explained. "Every dispute, every legal battle, every social slight, they were all carefully planned to maintain the illusion of enmity while disguising their joint criminal operations."

"And did the family members understand the true nature of this arrangement?" Mitchell asked.

"The inner circle absolutely knew," Eleanor confirmed. "They were raised within the covenant framework, indoctrinated from childhood to prioritize family loyalty above all."

When questioned about Elizabeth's investigation, Eleanor's testimony proved particularly damning. "Elizabeth discovered the covenant room through references in Thomas Mason's letters to Charlotte Rawlings, Elizabeth Rawlings' older sister. Once she accessed the surveillance archives, she methodically documented the connections between historical crimes and current operations, building a comprehensive case that would expose them."

"And the families' response to her investigation?" Mitchell asked.

"They classified her as an existential threat according to the covenant protocols and authorized her elimination." Eleanor's description matched the language found in the covenant amendments. "The same response they had implemented for previous threats, including the elimination of her sister Charlotte Rawlings in 1968."

Dr. Walker followed Eleanor. The man looked terrible. I figured he must have aged ten years since he'd been shot. Mitchell went easy on him and after ten short minutes, she excused him on medical grounds.

The last witness of the day was Sarah Walker. She testified as an expert witness about her father's research and the systematic attempts to silence both him and Elizabeth. Her account of Marshall's hospital hostage situation provided a concrete demonstration of the lengths to which the family representatives would go to protect the covenant's secrets.

"They weren't just concerned about criminal prosecution," she explained. "The covenant represented their foundational moral framework. Preserving it justified any action, including multiple murders."

As the proceedings adjourned for the day, Judge Holcomb instructed the federal marshals to maintain enhanced security for all the witnesses, including yours truly and Kate. The preliminary hearing would continue tomorrow with additional testimony about the Harris family's central role in designing and maintaining the criminal enterprise.

Outside the courthouse, media crews swarmed around us for comments from anyone connected to the case. Kate and I slipped out through the side exit, avoiding the press gauntlet.

"That went better than expected," Kate noted as we reached my car.

"It did," I said, as I started the engine, put the car in drive and pulled out onto the street.

"Where to now?" she asked.

"I'd like to see how Dr. Walker's doing," I replied. And so we drove to the hospital where Dr. Walker had been readmitted after his testimony—the exertion proving too taxing for his ongoing recovery. Sarah had accompanied him, her protective vigilance undiminished despite the increasing security surrounding the case.

"Harry, Kate," he said as we entered. "Thank you for coming. How nice it is to see you both."

We talked for a few moments, during which I asked him how he felt to which he replied, "Much better now the court understands. And Sarah did a wonderful job, don't you think?"

"Your testimony established the context perfectly," Kate assured him.

"Thank you," Walker replied, nodding. "Elizabeth would be pleased, I think.

As we prepared to leave, Sarah shared an update from the federal art crime division. "They've identified the descendants of twelve families whose artwork was looted during the Holocaust. Restitution proceedings have already begun for the pieces recovered from Mason's personal collection."

"That's good news," I said. "Elizabeth's primary objective was, I think, the return of the stolen artifacts to their rightful owners, not just punishing the families for the crimes. I..." I glanced at my watch and said, "I hate to run, but I must, so I'll see you tomorrow."

We were in my car when my phone rang. I glanced at the screen. "It's the chief," I said.

"Chief. What can I do for you?" I said.

"It went well today, so I hear. I thought you might be interested to know that Robert Harris is negotiating a comprehensive plea deal. Full cooperation in exchange for reduced charges and witness protection."

"How comprehensive?" Kate asked.

"Everything," Johnston replied. "He's prepared to dismantle the entire network in exchange for leniency."

"What about the patriarchs?" I asked.

"Still maintaining their innocence, despite the overwhelming evidence," Johnston replied. "Their attorneys are exploring mental competence strategies, suggesting they operated under covenant protocols without understanding the legal implications."

"That won't fly," Kate said confidently. "The surveillance recordings show clear awareness of the legal boundaries and their deliberate efforts to circumvent them."

"The prosecutors describe their case as 'biblically strong'" Johnston agreed, "which is appropriate given the covenant framework."

After Johnston hung up, Kate and I drove to the North Shore development site, where federal overseers had authorized the resumption of construction under modified plans. The excavation that had threatened family secrets would now proceed with archaeological oversight and the documentation of any new historical evidence the construction might uncover.

"Full circle," Kate observed as we watched workers carefully uncovering foundations of the old Mason textile mill. "The development project that got the old girl killed is now proceeding under federal oversight."

"Including a historical exhibition of the families' criminal activities integrated into the design," I added. "Elizabeth would appreciate the irony."

The site hummed with activity—construction crews working alongside archaeological teams, federal agents monitoring the excavation, and historical preservationists documenting discoveries. Elizabeth's vision was taking shape, though not precisely as she had planned.

The late afternoon sun cast long shadows across the excavation site. The machinery stood like stark sentinels on the crest of Cameron Hill. But I had a deep-seated feeling that somewhere beneath the dirt, more evidence remained buried, but would soon to be discovered as the scrapers continued to lower the Hill's profile.

As evening approached, we returned to the federal courthouse for a briefing on the next day's proceedings. Mitchell wanted to review the evidence of the Harris family's role before presenting it to the judge.

The courthouse had emptied of spectators, but security remained enhanced—federal marshals were posted at every entrance, identification checks carried out on all arriving and departing personnel, surveillance cameras monitoring all approaches and the surrounding streets and Miller Park beyond. The case had attracted national attention, with implications extending far beyond Chattanooga.

"Tomorrow, we establish the Harris dynasty as the architects of the entire system," Mitchell explained as we reviewed the documentation. "From William Harris, who designed the original covenant, through Robert Harris, and how they implemented it across seven decades. We will prove, beyond any doubt, that they were the true power behind both families."

"While publicly appearing to be mere employees," I added.

"The perfect cover," Mitchell agreed. "No one suspects the servant of controlling the master."

The evidence was compelling—covenant provisions granting William Harris enforcement authority, financial records showing his family's share in the proceeds, security protocols implemented across generations. William Harris had designed a criminal enterprise that positioned his descendants as the hidden power behind two of Chattanooga's most prominent families.

"The most damning evidence will come from Robert Harris himself," Mitchell continued. "His cooperation has provided confirmation of everything we suspected about the family's central role."

And so it went until, just about brain dead, I called a halt to the proceedings. "I think we've done enough for one day," I said. "I, for one, need a break. I'm going home. I'll see you tomorrow, Amy. You coming, Kate?"

SELF-PRESERVATION
Morning, The Next Day

THE FOLLOWING MORNING, the preliminary hearings resumed with, as expected, the focus on the Harris family's central role in the families' criminal enterprise. Robert Harris had been moved to the witness stand, his cooperation agreement completed overnight. His testimony would provide comprehensive confirmation of the covenant's implementation.

The courtroom was even more crowded than the previous day—additional media representatives, international observers, and family members. The atmosphere had shifted from initial shock to grim fascination as the full scope of the criminal enterprise emerged.

Harris testified with professional detachment, his military training evident in his precise descriptions and unemotional delivery. He detailed how his grandfather had designed the covenant, established the blood trust, and positioned himself as *the* enforcement authority while publicly appearing to be merely the Rawlings' head of security.

"The theatrical feud was central to the operation," Harris explained. "It distracted attention from the families' actual collaboration while allowing them to maintain control of key properties connected to their smuggling infrastructure."

"And your family's role in this arrangement?" Mitchell asked.

"We designed the system, implemented the security protocols, and maintained enforcement authority." Harris's candor was remarkable, his plea agreement having removed any incentive for evasion. "While publicly appearing to be employees of the Rawlings family, we actually maintained a controlling interest in their operations."

His testimony confirmed everything Dr. Walker had theorized about the true power structure—the Harris dynasty as architects of a criminal enterprise that positioned them as the hidden authority behind both prominent families.

"The covenant wasn't just a criminal agreement," Harris continued. "It created an alternate moral framework. Within that framework, eliminating threats like Elizabeth Rawlings wasn't considered murder. It was simply enforcing the covenant protocols."

This psychological insight aligned perfectly with Walker's analysis. The covenant was the foundational document that justified all criminal activities by establishing family honor as the highest code of ethics.

Harris proceeded to detail the security operations, the surveillance systems, evidence elimination protocols, and witness containment procedures. His matter-of-fact descriptions of 'existential threat responses' provided chilling confirmation of multiple murders justified by covenant loyalty.

"Elizabeth Rawlings was classified as an existential threat after she discovered the covenant room and surveillance archives," he explained. "According to established protocols, this allowed for her permanent elimination."

"And you implemented this authorization?" Mitchell asked.

"I gave no specific orders regarding Elizabeth Rawlings. I simply assigned the security team and coordinated with Lieutenant Marshall to ensure the investigation remained contained." Harris's admission was delivered without emotion. He shrugged. "It was standard procedure."

His testimony continued through the afternoon, establishing comprehensive documentation of the criminal enterprise's operations. Each revelation expanded the case beyond its original scope, demonstrating connections to officials and agencies throughout the Southeast.

After a thirty-minute break, when proceedings resumed, Harris testified about the blood trust's structure and operation.

"The trust wasn't just a holding company for properties," he explained. "It was the financial infrastructure that transformed proceeds from acquired assets into respectable family wealth."

"You mean it was laundered?" Mitchell asked.

"It was," he agreed.

Harris concluded his testimony, and, after another brief break, Judge Holcomb addressed the assembled attorneys. "Based on the evidence presented during these preliminary hearings, the court finds ample probable cause to support all charges against the defendants. This case will proceed to trial; scheduling yet to be determined given the perceived scope and complexity of the proceedings."

Outside the courthouse, the media crews struggled to summarize the day's revelations.

I found Kate conferring with two federal agents about what I didn't know or care. I'd had enough. As far as I was concerned, it was over until the trial, though God only knew when that would be.

"Harris's testimony was something, wasn't it?" she said as I joined her.

"Self-preservation," I said. "Maximizing his value to secure the best possible deal for himself."

"Professional to the end," Kate agreed.

As federal marshals prepared to transport Harris back into custody, he noticed me observing the process. Our eyes met briefly, and he nodded. I returned the nod, and, hands secured in front of him, he clambered awkwardly into the SUV.

I looked up at the night sky and took a deep breath. The night air carried the familiar scents of the river. I love that smell.

"What d'you think will happen to the blood trust properties?" Kate asked, breaking into my thoughts.

"Federal asset forfeiture, then likely a public auction," I replied. "Though there's discussion about preserving some of the historical buildings as is."

It was a week later when Amy Mitchell called to tell me the trial date had been set for Monday, September 10, 2007, and that the proceedings were expected to last several months. "But," she said, "it's not to be. The Mason and Rawlings patriarchs are negotiating a plea deal. It seems they've recognized the futility of fighting the overwhelming evidence. They're seeking leniency based on age and health considerations," she explained. "Though the surveillance recordings make justification difficult given their explicit authorization of Elizabeth's murder."

After ending the call, I shared this development with Kate. "The patriarchs have finally surrendered. They're wanting to make plea deals."

"I don't blame them," she said. "They have no chance of winning at trial. So, as you say, self-preservation, just like Harris."

Thus, it was that the families' carefully constructed world crumbled. Their financial assets were seized, their reputations destroyed, their carefully maintained theatrical feud exposed for the elaborate deception it was. Now those same families faced public retribution. I would have said atonement, but retribution sounds so much better, don't you think?

EPILOGUE

NEW BLOOD
   One Week Later

MY CONDO OFFERED the perfect vantage point for watching the morning light play across the Tennessee River. A week had passed since the Mason and Rawlings patriarchs had accepted plea agreements, marking the end of the covenant case as a criminal investigation. What remained now was the longer process of dismantling their empire, returning looted art to its rightful owners, and redistributing the assets acquired over three generations of criminal activity.

Kate arrived around nine with coffee and pastries, a weekend ritual we'd established during the investigation, but rarely had time to enjoy.

"Feeling strange?" she asked, joining me at the window.

"Like there's something I should be doing," I admitted. "After months of nonstop investigation, normal feels wrong somehow."

"They call it completion anxiety," Kate said, handing me a

coffee. "When you've been so focused on a case that finishing it feels disorienting. Kinda like post-partum depression."

The morning paper lay on my dining table, its front page dominated by coverage of the covenant case. "FAMILIES ACCEPT PLEA DEALS" announced the headline, with subheadings detailing asset forfeitures, restitution plans, and ongoing investigations into connected officials.

"Did you see the editorial?" Kate asked, gesturing to the paper. "It calls for a complete reexamination of Chattanooga's social history in light of the covenant revelations."

I nodded. "Rewriting that narrative won't happen overnight, if at all."

My phone rang. It was Chief Johnston calling with an update on internal department investigations triggered by Marshall's exposure. *Geez, I thought, does he never take a day off?*

"IA has identified seventeen officers with concerning connections to both families," he said. "It seems the corruption within the department runs deeper than we initially thought."

"No surprise there," I replied. "The families had seventy years to cultivate assets throughout local government. The department was/is an obvious target."

"The mayor's established a special commission to review corruption within the local law enforcement agencies. Sheriff White is not happy."

"I wondered about that," I said. "I wonder who Harris's contact in the sheriff's department was. It was never mentioned, was it? Had to be somebody, though. Harris was nothing if not professional."

"This is going to transform city governance for years to come, Harry," Johnston muttered. "And we still don't know who actually killed Elizabeth or Thorne."

"And we probably never will," I replied. "What we do know is that the poison was in Elizabeth's water glass, which she brought with her. We know that someone on one of the security teams implemented the murder under Robert Harris's direction, but we don't know who. We also know the patriarchs went along with it, and that Marshall helped cover it up. That's it."

Johnston was strangely quiet for a moment, then said, "I don't like loose ends, Harry."

"Neither do I, Chief, but that's where we're at."

"And Thorne?" he asked.

"Had to have been the security team that broke into his office," I said, "but which team…" I let my answer trail off.

After ending the call, I shared this update with Kate. Her expression reflected my own mixed feelings: satisfaction that justice was being seen to be done.

"Speaking of transformations," she said, pulling up photos on her phone, "have you seen the latest from the North Shore development?"

The images showed remarkable progress at the site. The foundations for the new Blue Cross Blue Shield buildings were already being poured. The archeological supervision had been withdrawn. And the building proper was about to begin.

"Sarah Walker called last night," I said in an effort to change the subject. "Her father is been released from the hospital and wants to meet us at the development site later this morning, around eleven. You up for that?"

"Sure," she replied. "But why?"

"Apparently, Dr. Walker wants to see the project taking shape," I told her. "Seems appropriate, I suppose, given his role in exposing the truth."

We finished breakfast and drove to the North Shore, where the development site had indeed been transformed from a crime scene into a construction project.

Dr. Walker was waiting for us near the main excavation area, seated in his wheelchair with oxygen support with Sarah beside him.

"They're making remarkable progress," Walker noted as we

approached, gesturing toward the construction. "Elizabeth would be pleased with how the project has evolved," he said.

"She would," I said, shivering slightly as a cool breeze wafted in from the river.

As noon approached, we were joined by an unexpected visitor. James Rawlings III arrived with his federal escort; protection provided as part of his plea agreements. His testimony against the family elders had earned him limited immunity, though he remained under supervision during the ongoing investigation.

"What the hell are you doing here, James?" I asked.

"I wanted to see what's happening with Grandmother's project," he explained, squinting, shading his eyes with his hand as he stared up at the building site.

"You've got a frickin' nerve," Kate said.

"So they say," he replied, turning to look at her.

She shook her head and turned her back on him.

Unperturbed, he turned to the Walkers and said, "Sarah, Dr. Walker. You're feeling better, I hope."

Walker merely nodded. Sarah said, "You asked about your grandmother's project. The modified plans preserve her core vision," she said stiffly.

James nodded, surveying the construction. "She was a wily old woman, wasn't she?"

"She planned for every contingency," Dr. Walker said. "Including her own death."

This assessment visibly affected James, who had clearly underestimated his grandmother's strategic foresight. "Yes, she knew they would kill her," he acknowledged softly. "But she did it anyway."

Two days later, Lieutenant Jack "Bull" Marshall agreed to comprehensive cooperation in exchange for witness protection. His testimony was expected to expose additional officers compromised through family connections, thus expanding the department's internal investigation.

Two days after that, a team of international art experts identified three more pieces from Mason's personal collection. It was determined that they had been looted from a private collection in Poland in 1939 and research was underway to find relatives of the family that had perished in the gas chambers at Buchenwald.

"Elizabeth's documentation is proving essential," Walker explained during a phone call. "Her research is allowing experts to make connections that might otherwise have taken years to establish."

"What happens now?"

"The larger reckoning continues, I suppose," I replied.

During the finalization of plea agreements, both patriarchs also admitted to authorizing Thorne's murder after discovering he'd uncovered documentation linking their families to Nazi collaboration. Robert Harris provided the names of the security team members who carried out that hit, and those individuals were now in federal custody facing charges of first-degree murder.

The academic community established a memorial scholarship in Thorne's name at the University of Tennessee Chattanooga, ensuring his contribution to exposing historical truth would be remembered alongside Elizabeth's. During the groundbreaking ceremony, Dr. Walker had specifically acknowledged his colleague's sacrifice, noting that Dr. Thorne's meticulous research provided crucial documentation of the families' historical crimes, and like Elizabeth, he paid the ultimate price for his commitment to the truth.

The following Sunday, as evening approached, we drove to the riverside park where, so I was told, Elizabeth spent a lot of time during her final months. A memorial service was planned for the following week, once Eleanor Rawlings and the minor family members not implicated in criminal activities—plus James III and Margaret Mason, who'd also made a deal—could arrange appropriate recognition of her work.

The park was quiet, and we sat on the steps and watched the Tennessee River as it flowed past, indifferent to the human dramas of thousands of years unfolding along its banks. The same waters that had carried Nazi gold seventy years earlier, now witnessed the dismantling of the empire built upon blood money.

ONE WEEK after the criminal case officially concluded in October 2007, exactly one year after it began, Kate and I attended the ground breaking ceremony for the historical exhibition center at the North Shore development named The Elizabeth Rawlings Center for Historical Truth. It was a fitting memorial to the woman whose death had catalyzed its transformation.

The ceremony attracted international media attention, with representatives from six Holocaust restitution organizations joining local officials and federal overseers. Dr. Walker delivered remarks from his wheelchair, providing context for the significance of what Elizabeth had uncovered.

"This center represents more than an exposition of criminal activity," he explained to the assembled journalists. "It documents how systematic deception shaped a city's development across three generations, creating social narratives built on elaborate theatrical performance rather than historical truth."

"Full circle," Kate observed as we walked back to my car.

"With her name on the building," I added, taking her hand in mine.

And so the story ended with the construction crews breaking ground on phase two of the North Shore Development, and I closed my eyes and once again I looked upon Elizabeth Rawlings' face as she whispered the words that started it all.

"Ask about the fire of '47."

KEEP READING for a look behind this book! Interesting facts, and additional information surrounding the story are on the next few pages. Enjoy!

AUTHOR'S NOTE

During the writing of "Blood in the Valley," I have taken some creative liberties with Chattanooga's Cameron Hill and underground spaces while staying true to the city's fascinating historical character. While Chattanooga does have underground passages, particularly in the downtown area, I've significantly expanded this network and connected it to Cameron Hill for narrative purposes. The extensive tunnel system described in the novel is fictional, though inspired by underground features found in many historical American cities.

Chattanooga, like many cities built in the 19th century, has undergone significant changes to its street levels over time. Parts of the original downtown were raised to combat flooding, creating underground spaces beneath the modern streets. These subterranean areas exist primarily as disconnected basement spaces rather than the comprehensive tunnel network depicted in this novel.

Chattanooga's Underground – The facts

Chattanooga has an underground street system known as "Underground Chattanooga." This subterranean network was created in the late 1800s following devastating floods, particularly the severe flood of 1867. To protect the city from future flooding, city planners raised the downtown street levels by 6 to 15 feet, effectively burying the first floors of many existing buildings.

As a result, former ground-level storefronts became basements, and new entrances were constructed on the upper floors. Many buildings maintained access to both levels, with the underground areas serving as storage or utility spaces. Some passageways connected buildings below street level.

The underground system spans approximately 10 blocks in downtown Chattanooga, primarily in the area between Market Street and the Tennessee River. While much of Underground Chattanooga remains inaccessible to the public today, portions have been rediscovered during modern construction and renovation projects.

Historical preservation efforts have increased interest in this hidden aspect of Chattanooga's past, with limited archaeological investigations and some building owners incorporating elements of the underground spaces into businesses. Unlike Seattle's Underground, which offers regular tours, Chattanooga's underground system is not fully developed as a tourist attraction, though occasional specialized tours have been offered.

Historical Note: Cameron Hill

Cameron Hill, a key element to the story, once stood as one of Chattanooga's most prominent geographical features—a steep,

330-foot hill overlooking the Tennessee River near the heart of downtown. Named for Scottish immigrant Paul Cameron, who settled the area in the early 19th century, the hill became home to Chattanooga's wealthiest residents in the late 1800s and early 1900s.

The hillside was developed into an exclusive residential neighborhood, adorned with Victorian mansions and stately homes that showcased the prosperity of Chattanooga's industrial elite. These families—made wealthy through manufacturing, banking, and commerce—created an enclave of privilege with panoramic views of the river and surrounding mountains.

By the mid-20th century, Cameron Hill had fallen into decline as wealthy residents moved to newer suburbs. In a controversial urban renewal project beginning in the late 1950s, the entire neighborhood was razed and much of the hill itself was physically lowered—an extraordinary engineering feat that forever altered Chattanooga's landscape. Approximately one-third of the hill was removed, and the soil was used for fill in other construction projects. This, too, was part of the inspiration for the story.

Today, the flattened remains of Cameron Hill host the head-quarters of Blue Cross Blue Shield of Tennessee and bear little resemblance to the commanding elevation that once defined Chattanooga's skyline. No original structures from the hill's heyday survive, making it one of the most dramatic examples of urban renewal's transformative—and often destructive—impact on American cities in the mid-20th century.

The complete removal of this once-prestigious neighborhood serves as a powerful reminder of how thoroughly a city's physical and social landscape can be altered, and how quickly history can be erased in the name of progress—themes that resonate throughout "Blood in the Valley."

From Blair Howard

The Harry Starke Genesis Series
9 Books in Series as of 2025

The Harry Starke Series
24 Books in Series as of 2025

The Lt. Kate Gazzara Murder Files
21 Books in Series as of 2025

Randall And Carver Mysteries
3 Books in Series as of 2025

The Peacemaker Series
3 Books in Series as of 2025

The O'Sullivan Chronicles: Civil War Series
5 Books in Series as of 2025

From Blair C. Howard

The Sovereign Star Series
7 Books in Series as of 2025

1st two books are also available in German

ABOUT THE AUTHOR

Blair Howard is a retired journalist turned novelist. He's the author of more than 65 novels including the international best-selling Harry Starke series of detective crime stories, the Lt. Kate Gazzara Police Procedural series, the Harry Starke Genesis series, and the Randall & Carver Mysteries. He's also the author of the Peacemaker series of international spy thrillers and five Civil War/Western novels.

If you enjoy reading Science Fiction thrillers, Mr. Howard has made his debut into the genre with, The Sovereign Stars Series under the name, Blair C. Howard.

www.BlairHowardBooks.com